La Muse

A Graphic Novel

Written by
Adi Tantimedh

Illustrated by
Hugo Petrus

with colors by
-3-

BIG
HEAD
PRESS ®

"Thoughtful Stories"
www.bigheadpress.com

La Muse

This is a work of fiction. All characters depicted herein are fictional and not intended to represent any actual persons, living or deceased.

Published under license by Big Head Press, P.O. Box 1853, Round Rock, TX 78680. Frank Bieser, publisher. Scott Bieser, editor. Cover design by Hugo Petrus, Adi Tantimedh and Scott Bieser.

ISBN: 978-0-9743814-6-6

Printed in Hong Kong

First Printing, October 2008

IS THAT HER? DO WE *KILL* HER NOW?

NO, THAT'S THE *SISTER!*

YOU HEARD THEM ON THEIR PHONES. SHE'S STILL ON HER WAY!

ALRIGHT, ALRIGHT!

JUST KEEP *COOL.* GOD NEEDS YOU TO KEEP COOL AND DO THIS RIGHT.

HEY! IS THAT HER? I THINK IT'S *HER!*

La Muse

PROLOGUE: "PEOPLE ARE PISSED AT YOU"

HEY LIBBY. SORRY I'M LATE.

THINGS RAN A LITTLE LATE.

WHICH "THINGS"?

WAS IT YOUR ADORING PUBLIC KISSING YOUR ASS OR WAS IT ONE OF *THESE?*

STORY:
ADI TANTIMEDH
ART:
HUGO PETRUS
COLORS:
-3-
LETTERS & EDITS:
SCOTT BIESER

DAMN, NEWS TRAVELS FAST.

WHO WOULD HAVE MISSED ANY OF *THAT?*

WHATEVER HAPPENED TO KEEPING THINGS *LOW-KEY?*

WHAT CAN I SAY? IT'S HARD TO BE LOW-KEY WHEN YOU'RE CHANGING THE WORLD.

ACTIVISM MAKES A LOT OF NOISE.

SUSAN—

DID YOU ORDER ME AN ICE COFF—?

AHA! THANKS!

SUSAN, WE *TALKED* ABOUT THIS! WHATEVER HAPPENED TO TAKING IT SLOW?

SIX MONTHS *IS* TAKING IT SLOW.

HI, ARE YOU SUSAN LA MUSE?

THAT'S ME.

I'M BRIAN, THIS IS MY PARTNER, JAKE.

WE JUST WANTED TO TELL YOU WE THINK YOU'RE TOTALLY *FABULOUS*.

WHY, *THANK YOU*.

EVERYTHING YOU'RE DOING IS GREAT.

HI, CAN YOU SIGN THIS FOR MY DAUGHTER? SHE'S SAVED *ALL* YOUR NEWS CLIPPINGS.

WOW! *COOL!* WHAT'S HER NAME?

PATTY.

THAT'S HER ALRIGHT.

LET'S DO IT!

SCREEEEEEE!

3

NO, THANK YOU.

REALLY.

DON'T WORRY, GUYS!

EVERYTHING'S COOL!

ANYWAY, BOTH DONNA KARAN *AND* GUCCI ARE AFTER ME TO MODEL FOR THEM, WHO DO YOU THINK I SHOULD PICK?

PERSONALLY, I'M MORE INTO ALEXANDER MCQUEEN, HE'S *FUNKIER*...

WHAT?

WE TELL THE COPS WHAT WE KNOW, WHICH ISN'T MUCH. IT WAS *ANOTHER* BUNCH OF ZEALOTS TRYING TO KILL HER.

JIHADISTS, ANTI-ABORTIONISTS, ANTI-GAY ACTIVISTS (THOUGH SHE'S NOT GAY), INTELLIGENT DESIGN FANATICS, THE KKK, NEO-NAZIS, YOU NAME IT, THEY WANT HER *DEAD*.

YEAH, TIM, I'M *OKAY*. DON'T WORRY ABOUT ME.

LET'S JUST SAY SUSAN INTRODUCED NEW MEANING TO THE TERM, *"TALK TO THE HAND"*.

NO, *REALLY!* I DON'T NEED TO GO TO THE HOSPITAL! THERE'S NO MEDICAL TREATMENT FOR "PISSED OFF"!

AND SUSAN? SHE'S HAVING THE TIME OF HER *LIFE*.

YEAH, YOU CAN MAKE ME FEEL BETTER. I'LL SEE YOU LATER, HONEY. 'BYE.

BUT THE TIME OF HER LIFE MEANS TURNING THE WORLD INTO HER PERSONAL FUCKING *PLAYGROUND*!

IT'S NOT A PLAYGROUND, IT'S A *SOCIAL EXPERIMENT*.

STOP READING MY MIND, *DAMMIT!*

SIX MONTHS! ALL IT TOOK WAS SIX MONTHS FOR YOU TO TURN THE WORLD UPSIDE DOWN! SIX MONTHS TO RUIN MY LIFE!

I THOUGHT I RUINED YOUR LIFE IN *FOUR WEEKS*.

OH, SHUT UP!

5

OKAY, LIBBY, WHAT ARE YOU SULKING ABOUT **NOW?**

AS IF YOU DON'T KNOW!

YOU HAD TO CHOOSE THE LOUDEST, MOST ATTENTION-GRABBING THING TO DO BACK AT THE CAFÉ, DIDN'T YOU!

MAYBE YOU **FORGOT,** BUT THOSE GUYS WERE OUT TO KILL YOU, ME, EVERYBODY ON THAT BLOCK.

AND YOU KILLED **THEM!** YOU DIDN'T **HAVE** TO!

NOBODY HAD A PROBLEM WITH IT. I DISHED TO THEM WHAT THEY WANTED TO DISH TO US. I CAN SAY IT WAS SELF-DEFENCE.

YOU COULD HAVE **FROZEN** THAT ROCKET! CAUGHT IT IN YOUR HAND! BUT NOOO! YOU HAD TO WIPE 'EM OFF THE FACE OF THE EARTH!

YOU ARE A GODDAMNED **SOCIOPATH!** AND YOU'VE MADE ME AN ACCESSORY!

SAY, LIB...

MAYBE YOU OUGHTTA SAY EVERYTHING YOU JUST SAID INTO THIS, ONLY **LOUDER.**

WHAT THE HELL IS **THAT?**

JUST A LISTENING DEVICE I FOUND UNDER YOUR STEERING WHEEL.

WHAT?!

IT WAS PUT THERE BY THE **GOVERNMENT GUYS** IN THE SEDAN FIFTY FEET BEHIND US.

DON'T' WORRY. I CHANGED THE OUTPUT SIGNAL. THEY'RE HEARING A LOOP OF THE **TOM WAITS** COVER OF THE LOVE THEME FROM "TITANIC".

NEEEEEEAAAARRRRRR... FAAAAAAAAARRRRR... WHERRRREEEEEVERRRRR YOU ARRRRRREEE...

JUST KILL ME...!

WE'RE BEING BUGGED BY THE GOVERNMENT?!

YUP! OUR PHONES, OUR EMAILS, BANK ACCOUNTS, CREDIT CARDS...

CHILL, LIB! I CAN OVERRIDE THEM AND THEY WON'T EVER HEAR ANYTHING *PRIVATE*.

OH GOD ...

HOW DID MY LIFE COME TO THIS...?

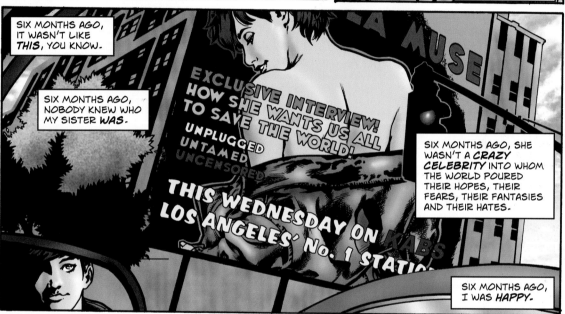

SIX MONTHS AGO, IT WASN'T LIKE *THIS*, YOU KNOW.

SIX MONTHS AGO, NOBODY KNEW WHO MY SISTER *WAS*.

EXCLUSIVE INTERVIEW! HOW SHE WANTS US ALL TO SAVE THE WORLD!

UNPLUGGED UNTAMED UNCENSORED

THIS WEDNESDAY ON KABS LOS ANGELES' No. 1 STATION

LA MUSE

SIX MONTHS AGO, SHE WASN'T A *CRAZY CELEBRITY* INTO WHOM THE WORLD POURED THEIR HOPES, THEIR FEARS, THEIR FANTASIES AND THEIR HATES.

SIX MONTHS AGO, I WAS *HAPPY*.

CHAPTER ONE: "SIX MONTHS AGO, WHEN I WAS HAPPY..."

SIX MONTHS AGO, I WAS JUST ANOTHER AGENT AT THE *PRITKIN AGENCY*, HUSTLING DEALS FOR A-LIST ACTORS, WRITERS AND DIRECTORS, SWIMMING IN THE SHARK-INFESTED WATERS OF HOLLYWOOD.

MORNING, ANIJA!

ER, *HI*, LIBBY.

WHAT'S GOING ON? DID AN **A-LISTER** GET CAUGHT WITH A DEAD HOOKER IN VEGAS OR SOMETHING?

IT'S... SOMETHING HAPPENED IN **LONDON**...

WAS IT A **BOMB?**

SOMETHING LIKE THAT...

..ARE STILL COMING IN FROM LONDON INVOLVING AN ATTEMPTED SUICIDE BOMBING...

THIS AMATEUR VIDEO FOOTAGE SHOWS AN AMERICAN WOMAN AT THE CENTER OF THE INCIDENT...

HUH.

AN AMERICAN **HAS** TO BE INVOLVED IF THEY'RE MAKING A BIG DEAL OUT OF IT...

FFFFFFFHHHT!

AW, C'MON, SUSAN, DON'T BE SUCH A **B(BLEEP!)**

GET THAT OUT OF MY FACE, TODD!

THE INCIDENT OCCURRED AT A PROTEST AGAINST CORPORATE EXPLOITATION OF THE THIRD WORLD, WHERE OVER 5,000 PEOPLE WERE PRESENT.

WHO-?

WHA-?

HUH-?

NOT **EVERYTHING** HAS TO REVOLVE AROUND YOU TRYING TO GET "COOL" FOOTAGE FOR YOUR VLOG!

YEAH, BUT WHAT ARE YOU IN SUCH A **RUSH** ABOUT?

THE WOMAN HAS BEEN IDENTIFIED AS **SUSAN LA MUSE**, A POLITICAL ACTIVIST AND CAMPAIGNER FROM NEW YORK.

THE FOLLOWING FOOTAGE MAY CONTAIN **DISTURBING** MATERIAL ...

09/17/04 15:17:42

afalgar Square, London

I **TOLD** YOU! THERE'S A GUY WITH A **BOMB** HERE!

8

9

STOP FILMING ME, TODD!

(BLEEP) ME!

THIS CAN'T BE REAL!

HEY, LIBBY...

ABS

ISN'T THAT *YOUR* SISTER?

SHIT.

AHH, THAT SUSAN! IT'S A HOAX! GOTTA BE! VIRAL VIDEO!

SHE PULLS CRAZY SHIT ALL THE TIME!

---THE MAN WHO SHOT THE VIDEO, TODD BERGERSON, HAS *DENIED* IT WAS A HOAX.

MORE FOOTAGE AND PHOTOGRAPHS TAKEN FROM TOURISTS' AND PASSERSBY'S CAMERAPHONES SEEM TO SUPPORT HIS CLAIM...

ANYWAY, WE HAVE WORK TO DO!

JEFF! HAS WARNERS SENT OVER CHAD WILMER'S CONTRACT YET?

BY NOON THAT DAY, *THAT VIDEO* HAD SHOWN UP ON ALL THE TV CHANNELS AND BEEN WATCHED BY OVER *TWO MILLION PEOPLE* ON THE INTERNET.

MY LIFE WAS A SMOLDERING RUIN, BUT I WAS IN *DENIAL*, I GUESS. I WAS TRYING TO CARRY ON LIKE NORMAL, BUT THAT WAS TOUGH WHEN EVERYONE IN TOWN FOUND OUT SHE WAS MY SISTER.

SO WHAT ABOUT THE CLAUSE WHERE--? YES, IT'S MY SISTER! NO, I DON'T KNOW WHERE SHE IS! WHY ARE WE *DISCUSSING*-?

MY BOSS JUST STEPPED IN. I'LL HAVE TO CALL YOU BACK.

HOW ARE YOU HOLDING UP, LIBBY? I'M SURPRISED YOU DIDN'T TAKE THE DAY OFF TO GO FIND SUSAN.

AHH, YOU KNOW ME -- GOTTA LOOK AFTER THE CLIENTS!

BESIDES, I'LL BET SHE GOT THE HELL OUTTA ENGLAND, CONSIDERING HOW MUCH *TROUBLE* SHE'S IN...

SHE SAVED A LOT OF LIVES TODAY.

THE POLICE JUST ROUNDED UP THE REST OF THE TERROR CELL IN LONDON.

EVEN MODERATE MUSLIMS ARE PRAISING HER REMARKS.

WELL, BULLY FOR *HER*. SO SHE'S A HERO.

AND I CAN'T *BELIEVE* YOU'RE LEAVING HER TO FEND FOR HERSELF LIKE THIS.

SHE CAN TAKE CARE OF HERSELF!

YOU'RE *MISSING THE BIG PICTURE.*

WITH THAT ONE VIDEO, YOUR SISTER HAS BECOME THE MOST FAMOUS PERSON ON THE *PLANET* IN LESS THAN TWO HOURS. YOU COULDN'T BUY THAT PUBLICITY IF YOU HAD MORE MONEY THAN *GOD*.

BY LUNCHTIME, EVERYONE ON EARTH IS GOING TO WANT A PIECE OF HER.

DICK-- WHAT-- DICK, WHAT ARE YOU *SAYING*? SHE'S NOT AN ACTRESS--!

SO? WE REPRESENT AUTHORS, SPORTS STARS AND EX-PRESIDENTS. WHATEVER SUSAN IS, THE PRITKIN AGENCY CAN REPRESENT HER INTERESTS AS WELL.

I'VE BEEN STUDYING THAT TAPE FOR THE LAST *HOUR*.

THE CAMERA LOVES HER.

WE NEED TO SIGN HER BEFORE CAA, ICM OR WILLIAM MORRIS GET THEIR HANDS ON HER.

AND AS HER SISTER, THAT GIVES YOU AN EDGE. THAT GIVES *US* AN EDGE.

SO THAT'S HOW I WAS *ORDERED* TO DROP EVERYTHING AND GET ON THE FIRST PLANE TO NEW YORK TO FIND HER.

DICK MADE IT VERY CLEAR THAT IF I *DIDN'T*, HE WOULD HAVE TO RETHINK HOW SERIOUS I WAS ABOUT MY CAREER IN THE INDUSTRY. AND YOU DO *NOT* WANT TO GET BLACKBALLED BY *DICK PRITKIN!*

WHAT **AMAZES** ME IS THAT NO ONE ASKED ME WHERE SUSAN GOT HER POWERS FROM OR IF I HAD ANY OF MY OWN. AND THANK GOD FOR THAT.

ALL I HAD TO WORRY ABOUT WAS **FINDING** HER.

NOW, THERE WAS NO WAY SHE WOULD HAVE STAYED IN ENGLAND AFTER THAT STUNT. I'D GET THE HELL OUT OF DODGE, TOO, AND GO TO THE **LAST PLACE** ANYONE WOULD THINK TO LOOK FOR ME.

IN SUSAN'S CASE, SHE HAS A **LOT MORE** PLACES TO CHOOSE FROM THAN ANYONE ELSE.

HI **THERE** !

AND WHAT'S A GOOD-LOOKIN' GUY LIKE **YOU** DOING ALL ALONE IN A PLACE LIKE **THIS?**

AS FOR ME, I WAS BACK IN **NEW YORK,** WHERE SUSAN AND I GREW UP. I TOLD DICK SHE MIGHT FLEE BACK HERE, BUT I WAS REALLY LOOKING FOR AN EXCUSE TO GET OUT OF LA BEFORE PEOPLE STARTED **HOUNDING** ME ABOUT HER.

OH.

I KINDA LET SLIP THAT YOU WERE SUSAN'S SISTER, AND MY BOSS WAS ON ME LIKE MADONNA ON AN **AFRICAN ORPHAN**.

SHE EVEN CALLED **YOUR** BOSS, TOLD HIM SUSAN COULD USE A GOOD P.R. FIRM, AND DICK AGREED!

NO, I'M IN **SUSAN'S** APARTMENT ON THE LOWER EAST SIDE. I HAVE A KEY.

IS SHE **THERE?**

'COURSE NOT! I HAVE **NO IDEA** WHERE SHE'S GONE!

LISTEN, BABE. I'M COMING OUT TO NEW YORK TONIGHT, TOO. MAYBE WE CAN HAVE **BREAKFAST** IN THE MORNING.

AWW... TIM, YOU DIDN'T HAVE TO COME OUT HERE FOR **ME**...

ER, **FULL DISCLOSURE**, BABE...

MY BOSS **ORDERED** ME TO FLY OUT. SHE WANTS ME TO SIGN SUSAN AS A CLIENT.

WELL, MARIAM AND DICK USED TO BE **MARRIED**, SO THEY'RE KEEPING IT ALL IN THE FAMILY...

THEY'RE THE **FUCKIN'** KING AND QUEEN OF **EVIL**, AND WE'RE THEIR FOOTSOLDIERS!

GEE, THAT MAKES ME FEEL A LOT BETTER.

CALL ME WHEN YOU GET IN?

YOU BET.

LOVE YA.

LOVE YOU, **TOO.** LATER.

(CLICK!)

SIGH!

OKAY, TIME TO GET IN TOUCH.

I **HATE** DOING THIS.

SUSAN...

SUSAN!!

HMM? WHU?

WHERE THE HELL ARE YOU?

JEEZ, DIAL IT *DOWN*, LIB...!

WE GOTTA TALK! AS IN, *NOW*! WHERE ARE YOU?

I'M IN THE *NORTH POLE*.

I'LL 'PORT YOU OVER.

NO! WAIT-!

YAAAAAAAAAAAAAAAH!

RELAX, LIBBY! I'M GOING TO WARM THE AIR AROUND YOU!

I SEE YOU DIDN'T WASTE ANY *TIME* FINDING A FUCK-BUDDY.

BEST WAY TO RELIEVE STRESS!

HIS NAME'S *AMORAK*. MEANS "SPIRIT OF THE WOLF". AND HE'S DEFINITELY A WOLF. AWOOOO!

AWOOOOO!

THREESOME?

NO, DUDE. SORRY. MY SISTER'S A *PRUDE*. WHY DON'T YOU GO INSIDE?

I'LL JOIN YOU LATER.

AWWW!

I'M *NOT A PRUDE!*

ANYWAY! CAN WE GET BACK *ON-TOPIC* HERE?

YOU'VE MANAGED TO MESS UP MY LIFE WITHOUT EVEN *TRYING!*

THE STUFF YOU PULLED USED TO BE *SMALL* ENOUGH THAT NOBODY NOTICED! BUT *THIS TIME,* YOU REALLY HAVE LANDED US IN THE SHIT!

WHAT DID YOU THINK YOU WERE *DOING?*

I LET *TODD* TALK ME INTO TAKING HIM TO LONDON FOR THE WEEK SO HE COULD FILM THE PROTEST FOR HIS STUPID VIDEO BLOG.

OKAY! I *ADMIT* IT! I FUCKED UP!

I CAUGHT THE *THOUGHTS* OF THE GUY WITH THE BOMB.

WHAT DO YOU *EXPECT* ME TO DO?

LET HIM BLOW UP TRAFALGAR SQUARE AND *KILL* THE PEOPLE WHO WERE THERE?

THE QUESTION IS WHAT DO WE DO *NOW?*

WELL, SEEING AS THE CAT'S OUTTA THE *BAG*...

I DON'T WANT ANYONE FINDING OUT WE'RE *ALIENS.*

TECHNICALLY, WE'RE *HUMAN.* OUR BODIES ARE HUMAN.

BUT *YOU'RE* THE ONE WHO FLIES AND IS INVULNERABLE!

DON'T KNOCK IT TILL YOU'VE *TRIED* IT, LIB.

IF I DON'T SIGN YOU TO MY AGENCY, I LOSE MY *JOB.*

SERIOUSLY?

17

YOU REALLY DON'T *GET* IT, DO YOU? YOU'RE *BIG* NOW!

EVERYBODY, AND I MEAN *EVERYBODY*, WANTS A PIECE OF YOU.

I HAVE A JOB THAT I *LIKE*, WITH A SMALL-BUT-GROWING LIST OF MAJOR CLIENTS THAT I WORK MY ASS OFF FOR.

OH. HUH.

OKAY, *FINE!*

CUT IT *OUT!*

I AM PUTTING MYSELF IN YOUR *CAPABLE* HANDS, SO YOU CAN *KEEP* YOUR JOB AND YOUR VALUABLE SOUTH-ERN CALIFORNIAN LIFESTYLE!

I WILL DO EVERYTHING YOU SAY, SO THAT WE SAFEGUARD OUR *SECRET!* AND THE SECRET OF WHAT I'M *REALLY* CAPABLE OF! IS THAT WHAT YOU WANTED TO HEAR?

ENOUGH! GET *UP* ALREADY!

OKAY. WE HAVE TO SQUARE THINGS WITH THE AUTHORITIES IN *LONDON*, AND LET'S START SOME DAMAGE CONTROL –

I HEAR YA.

WHERE ARE YOU *GOING?*

TO GIVE AMORAK A *GOODBYE BONK.* I'LL JUST BE A FEW MINUTES.

MMMMM!

AWOOOOO!

GIGGLE!

AWWWOOOOOO!

HA HA HA HA HA!

I TOLD *TIM* TO MEET US IN LONDON. FROM THE MEDIA FEEDING FRENZY, WE WERE GOING TO *NEED* HIM.

DICK PULLED STRINGS AND GOT SUSAN AN EXPENSIVE *LAWYER*, BUT IT WAS JUST A FORMALITY TO PROVE SHE HAD NOTHING TO DO WITH THE TERRORISTS. AND ANYWAY, TO THE PUBLIC, SHE WAS THEIR NEW *HERO*.

OOOKAY...

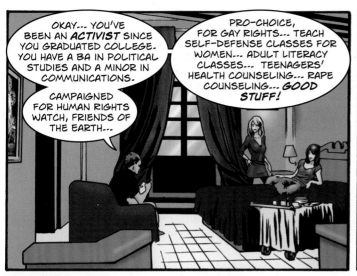

OKAY... YOU'VE BEEN AN *ACTIVIST* SINCE YOU GRADUATED COLLEGE. YOU HAVE A BA IN POLITICAL STUDIES AND A MINOR IN COMMUNICATIONS.

CAMPAIGNED FOR HUMAN RIGHTS WATCH, FRIENDS OF THE EARTH...

PRO-CHOICE, FOR GAY RIGHTS... TEACH SELF-DEFENSE CLASSES FOR WOMEN... ADULT LITERACY CLASSES... TEENAGERS' HEALTH COUNSELING... RAPE COUNSELING... *GOOD STUFF!*

TIM DOESN'T KNOW ABOUT THE *ALIEN THING* AND THAT WAS HOW IT WAS GOING TO *STAY.*

AND NOW: *THE MAKEOVER.*

IS THIS *REALLY* NECESSARY?

YOU GOTTA LOOK *GOOD* FOR YOUR FIRST PRESS CONFERENCE.

SHE NEEDS A *FACE MASK,* YES.

OPEN THE PORES UP, LET THEM *BREATHE.*

MUDPACK, PEEL AWAY ALL THOSE *DEAD CELLS.*

YOU GOT *GOOD SKIN.* WE NEED IT TO *GLOW.*

BUT THIS MAD-STRAGGLY HAIR SIMPLY *WON'T DO!*

FOR A *JUNKIE* ON AVENUE D, FINE! BUT FOR A STAR, NO!

THANK GOD YOU BROUGHT HER TO ME BEFORE IT WAS *TOO LATE,* DARLINGS!

GO FOR A FRINGE, PERHAPS A BOB, BIT ANDROGYNOUS, FRAME THE FACE AND CHEEKBONES!

HELLO, I'M *STILL HERE.*

NOW, THE BOOBIES: TOO SMALL, TOO LIKE A *BOY'S.* I SUGGEST IMPLANTS, FIRMER, MORE RIPE --

GRAB ME AND YOU DIE!

CLAUDE, DON'T *GO THERE.* JUST THE HAIRCUT AND THE FACIAL, OKAY?

19

WHY CAN'T I WEAR MY *OWN* STUFF?

DARLING, WHAT MAKES A *STAR* IS PEOPLE EITHER WANT TO BE YOU OR FUCK YOU! OR *BOTH!*

AT THE VERY *LEAST,* THEY WANT YOU TO BE THEIR BEST FRIEND!

WE CAN'T HAVE YOU TALKING ABOUT SOCIAL JUSTICE AND SAVING THE WORLD DRESSED LIKE A *VIDEO STORE CLERK!*

BUT IT'S JUST A JACKET AND JEANS.

OR A REFUGEE FROM *CBGB'S* CLOSING NIGHT!

WELL, I'M NOT WEARING A DRESS. I *FLY* A LOT.

DAMPEN DOWN THE FEMININITY? GOING FOR THE *SEXY TOMBOY?* I CAN DIG IT, DARLING!

I *HATE* ALL THE PREENING! I'VE ALWAYS BEEN A "THROW IT ON IF IT LOOKS DECENT" GIRL!

THAT MUCH IS *OBVIOUS!*

ALRIGHT, THEN! WHAT DO YOU *LIKE?* DRAW ME A *PICTURE,* DARLING!

LEATHER.

NOW WE'RE TALKING!

I WAS SO *CAUGHT UP* IN THINGS, I SHOULD HAVE WONDERED WHY EVERYTHING WENT SO SMOOTHLY, RIGHT UP TO THE PRESS CONFERENCE.

YOU COULD SAY IT WAS SUSAN'S COMING OUT PARTY.

OKAY, THE REPORTERS ARE SITTING DOWN NOW. LET'S TAKE IT *SLOW*.

STAY CALM, SUSAN. DON'T *WORRY*, THIS IS JUST LIKE FACING A PIT OF HUNGRY TIGERS.

NOT *FUNNY*, TIM.

YOU KNOW, LIBBY, I *SEE* IT NOW... ALL THIS MACHINERY TO MAKE A PUBLIC FIGURE...

IT'S LIKE A *PROJECT* JUST LIKE MOM AND DAD'S PEOPLE LIKE TO GET INTO.

I GUESS YOU COULD SAY THAT.

BUT I ALSO REALIZED SOMETHING *ELSE*...

CELEBRITY IS A *WEAPON*.

IT'S THE BEST SWORD AN *ACTIVIST* COULD ASK FOR.

IT'S LIKE AN E-TICKET TO KICKING IT *UP* A NOTCH.

OKAY, YOU'RE *ON*. DEEP BREATH, SUSAN!

SO YEAH.

LET'S DO "CELEBRITY".

THIS IS FROM HER **FIRST** PRESS CONFERENCE SIX MONTHS AGO...

WHERE DID MY POWERS **COME** FROM? I DON'T KNOW. I REALLY **DON'T**.

I JUST SUDDENLY **HEARD** THE GUY'S THOUGHTS. HE HAD A **BOMB**. I KNEW I HAD TO STOP HIM.

I DIDN'T EVEN **THINK** ABOUT DYING, YOU KNOW? I WAS JUST TRYING TO STOP HIM. EVERYTHING THAT HAPPENED... JUST **HAPPENED**. IT WAS PRETTY WILD.

...NO, I **DON'T** THINK GOD GAVE ME THESE POWERS.

REALLY, I JUST DON'T **BELIEVE** THERE'S A GUY IN THE SKY WITH A BEARD WHO HATES GAYS.

SHE'S AN **ATHEIST**. THAT'S THE FIRST CLUE THAT SHE'S NOT ON OUR SIDE.

A RECENT POLL SHOWS THAT 4% OF THE PUBLIC THINKS SHE'S THE **ANTICHRIST**.

YET HER POPULARITY IS STILL **GROWING**.

GENTLEMEN, IT IS MY CONCLUSION THAT SHE POSES A **GRAVE DANGER** TO EVERYTHING WE HOLD DEAR.

Chapter 2: ENTER THE HATERS

AGENT **VENKOW**, IF YOU COULD TALK US THROUGH THE SURVEILLANCE MATERIAL YOU'VE GATHERED...?

THESE ARE PICTURES OF THE SUBJECT AND HER SISTER VISITING THEIR **PARENTS'** GRAVE IN NEW YORK, A WEEK AFTER HER FIRST PRESS CONFERENCE.

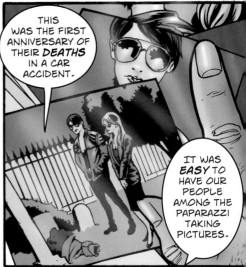

THIS WAS THE FIRST ANNIVERSARY OF THEIR **DEATHS** IN A CAR ACCIDENT.

IT WAS **EASY** TO HAVE OUR PEOPLE AMONG THE PAPARAZZI TAKING PICTURES.

"I BELIEVE THEY STAGED THIS EVENT FOR THE MEDIA TO BOOST HER IMAGE."

I CAN'T **BELIEVE** WE'RE ACTUALLY DOING THIS AS A MEDIA EVENT!

HEY, TIM SAID IT'D BE **GOOD PR.** "SISTERS UNITED", "LOVING DAUGHTERS" AND ALL THAT SHIT. WHAT THE HELL.

Peter and Marianne La Muse, 1953 – 2003 Out of space, out of time, But not out of our hearts

UNLESS YOU WANT TO TELL EVERYONE THAT MOM AND DAD AREN'T REALLY DEAD AND WE'RE **ALIENS.**

YEAH, RUB IT **IN!** WHERE THE HELL **ARE** MOM AND DAD ANYWAY?

I DUNNO. TRIED CONTACTING 'EM, BUT I WAS TOLD THEY WERE OFF EXPLORING ANOTHER UNIVERSE.

GREAT! THEIR DAUGHTER HAS THROWN THIS WORLD INTO TURMOIL AND THEY'RE OFF PLAYING SPACE TOURISTS!

WHOA! DO YOU FEEL THAT?

WHAT?

TIME JUST STOPPED.

AGENT VENKOW, I HAVE TO ASK. IS IT REALLY **NECESSARY** TO MONITOR HER THAT MUCH?

I WAS SKEPTICAL WHEN THE **PRESIDENT** ORDERED ME TO KEEP AN EYE ON HER, BUT I'VE CHANGED MY MIND.

SHE'S A KNOWN ACTIVIST AND **TROUBLE-MAKER.**

HER ANTI-CORPORATE, ANTI-CAPITALIST VIEWS ARE WELL-DOCUMENTED.

HAVING POWERS MAKES HER EVEN **MORE** OF A THREAT.

BUT DON'T YOU THINK SHE MIGHT BE **SEDUCED** BY FAME AND FORTUNE, AND **CEASE** TO BE A THREAT?

THAT'S THE BEST-CASE SCENARIO, SIR, BUT I DON'T **THINK** SO.

"SHE'S BEEN VISITING ALL THE PLACES IN THE THIRD WORLD THAT HAD VICTIMS OF **LANDMINES** AND **RESTORING** THEIR MISSING LIMBS."

"AND AFTER HER TOUR OF THE AIDS HOTSPOTS IN AFRICA, THE **WHO** REPORTED **NO NEW** CASES OF HIV INFECTION, AND MORE AND MORE CASES OF **REMISSION** FROM AIDS AND HIV ON THE CONTINENT."

29

SO SHE'S A BLEEDING-HEART *DO-GOODER.* THAT HARDLY WARRANTS GOING AFTER HER...

THERE'S *MORE*...

"THE DAY SHE FOILED THE LONDON BOMBING AND FLED THE SCENE, SATELLITES PHOTOGRAPHED AN ANOMALY OVER THE NORTH POLE. THE HOLE IN THE OZONE LAYER BEGAN TO *SHRINK* EXPONENTIALLY. ICE CAPS THAT WERE MELTING FROZE AGAIN."

"A LOCAL INUIT MAN CLAIMED TO HAVE *MET* HER UP THERE."

"I DON'T BELIEVE IN COINCIDENCE, AND HER *NOT* TAKING CREDIT FOR THIS DISTURBS ME EVEN *MORE*."

THINK ABOUT IT: SHE SAVED THE WORLD WITHOUT *TELLING* ANYONE.

I THINK THESE WERE JUST *BABY-STEPS.* SHE'S GETTING MORE AMBITIOUS.

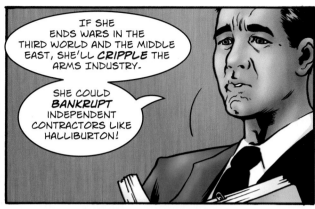

SHE HAS CALLED FOR THE BOYCOTT OF COCA COLA FOR CORRUPT ENVIRONMENTAL PRACTICES -- IT *WORKED!*

SHE HAS ADVISED *HEDGE FUNDS* ON WHAT CORPORATIONS TO BET NEGATIVE ON, AND THEY DID IT!

IF SHE ENDS WARS IN THE THIRD WORLD AND THE MIDDLE EAST, SHE'LL *CRIPPLE* THE ARMS INDUSTRY.

SHE COULD *BANKRUPT* INDEPENDENT CONTRACTORS LIKE HALLIBURTON!

WE STILL *DON'T* KNOW EXACTLY WHAT HER POWERS *ARE.*

WHAT IF SHE DECLARES WAR ON US?

SHE DOES NOT SERVE THE SOCIAL ORDER. SHE'S OUT TO *OVERTURN* IT.

THAT'S WHY WE HAVE TO SHUT HER DOWN.

NOW, I TOOK THE LIBERTY OF TRYING OUT SOME PRE-EMPTIVE *STRIKES* OVER THE LAST FIVE MONTHS...

"AFTER THE SUBJECT RETURNED TO *NEW YORK,* WE TAILED HER TO A SHOPPING TRIP IN *SOHO.* WE DECIDED IT WOULD BE BEST TO MAKE IT LOOK LIKE A *CAR ACCIDENT.*"

BATTERING RAM TO MOTHER HEN, TARGET *ACQUIRED.* OVER.

REMEMBER, YOU ONLY HAVE *ONE SHOT.* OVER.

Griswo
Refriger
Brr-r-r-r-

CLOTHES! MAKE-UP! SHOES! I CAN'T **BELIEVE** HOW MUCH SHOPPING A CELEBRITY NEEDS TO DO!

YOU COULD HAVE JUST GOTTEN CLAUDE'S TEAM TO BUY IT FOR YOU.

HE'D PUT ME IN A CORSET AND GARTER BELT IF HE HAD HIS WAY.

I'M AN ACTIVIST, NOT A **PORN** STAR.

COULD'VE FOOLED ME.

I SWEAR, CLAUDE GOES **OVERBOARD** WITH HIS DRAG QUEEN FETISH.

SUSAN, IS IT ME OR ARE YOU KIND OF **STRESSED**?

DAMN STRAIGHT! I **HATE** SHOPPING! I GOTTA BUY SOME CIGARETTES!

OKAY, MEET US AT THE STORE ACROSS THE STREET.

SHE'S CROSSING THE STREET NOW!

BATTERING RAM, YOU ARE GOOD TO **GO!** REMEMBER TO DUMP THE CAR TEN BLOCKS AWAY. WE'LL PICK YOU UP THERE!

MAKE SURE MY **FAMILY** GETS THE MONEY!

I SWEAR, SHE'S SUCH A **DRAMA QUEEN**...

THAT'S WHAT MAKES HER A STAR.

YEAH, BUT --

OH MY GOD! SUSAN!

LOOK OUT!

SUSAN!

MOTHERFUCKER WANTED TO **KILL** ME. READ IT OFF HIS BRAIN.

HKKKK---!

DUDE, YOUR AIRBAG DIDN'T OPEN. AND YOU KNOW YOUR BRAKES WERE **CUT**?

THEY SET YOU UP TO TAKE THE FALL

AAAARG-GGGH!

SUSAN, AN AMBULANCE IS COMING...

HE'LL BE **DEAD** BEFORE IT GETS HERE.

OH, JESUS...

AKKK!

ARGH!

AAAAA!

UKKK!

HMM... HEAD TRAUMA, FRACTURED SKULL, FRACTURED STERNUM, RUPTURED SPLEEN, INTERNAL BLEEDING, FRACTURED PELVIS...

DON'T BE SUCH A **BABY**! I ALREADY SHUT OFF YOUR PAIN CENTER!

AND VOILA! GOOD AS NEW!

YOU— YOU HAVE **SAVED** MY LIFE!

YEAH, YEAH, DON'T SWEAT IT.

JUST STAY IN MY GUEST ROOM, SAVE YOUR MONEY. AND I CAN KEEP AN *EYE* ON YOU WHEN YOU'RE OUT THERE.

YOU SHOULD JUST MOVE TO *LA.*

NO *WAY!* YOU KNOW HOW LONG IT TOOK ME TO FIND A RENT-STABILIZED APARTMENT IN NEW YORK?

YOUR CALL.

MOSQUITO TO MOTHER HEN. TARGET *ACQUIRED.* I AM GOOD TO GO. OVER.

FIRE AT WILL. OVER.

I'M *NOT* GIVING UP THIS PLACE IF I CAN HELP IT...

WHAT THE HELL?!

WHAT *IS* IT, MOSQUITO? OVER!

SHE CAN **SEE** ME!

SHE'S **900** FEET **AWAY** AND SHE'S LOOKING RIGHT **AT** ME!

MOSQUITO! RESPOND! TAKE ANOTHER SHOT!

OR GET OUT OF THERE! MOSQUITO?

PTUI!

UGK-!

MOSQUITO? **MOSQUITO!**

C'EST LA GUERRE, PAL.

DID YOU JUST **SPIT** OUT THE WINDOW?

ER, YEAH.

THAT IS SO GROSS! WHAT ARE YOU, **TWELVE?**

MOTHER HEN TO MOSQUITO, **COME IN!**

MOSQUITO? DO YOU **COPY?**

"WE HAD A CLEAN-UP CREW THERE WITHIN **MINUTES** TO TAKE THE BODY AWAY AND SANITIZE THE SCENE."

AGENT VENKOW, THAT'S *TWO* FAILED OPERATIONS THAT COST YOU AS MANY PEOPLE. TELL US WHY WE HAVEN'T REPLACED YOU.

WE'RE ATTACKING ON *MORE* THAN ONE FRONT.

THAT INCLUDES CUT-OUTS. WE'RE CREATING *NEGATIVE STORIES* ABOUT HER, SCANDALS, DESIGNED TO DISCREDIT HER.

"THAT MEANS CULTIVATING TIES WITH *JOURNALISTS* WILLING TO REPORT WHATEVER WE FEED THEM.

LA MUSE? I *HATE* HER!

DO YOU KNOW WE WERE AT *BENNINGTON* TOGETHER?

"CHIEF AMONG THEM IS *NAOMI PINNEY*, A FREELANCE ENTERTAINMENT JOURNALIST IN LOS ANGELES."

SO I HEARD.

WE WERE BEST BUDS, UNTIL THE "DRESSED TO GET LAID" PARTY IN SOPHOMORE YEAR! SHE HAD SEX WITH *MY* BOYFRIEND!

WELL, HE WASN'T MY BOYFRIEND, NOT YET! I *WAS* GONNA BAG HIM! ONLY SHE BEAT ME TO IT!

OKAY, SHE *DIDN'T* KNOW I WAS ATTRACTED TO HIM, BUT THAT'S NOT THE POINT! THAT *SLUT!*

SO WHAT DO YOU WANT ME FOR?

WELL, MY ORGANIZATION IS GATHERING SOME *DIRT* ON HER, AND WE WOULD BE HAPPY TO *COMPENSATE* YOU FOR GETTING THOSE STORIES OUT THERE.

HELL, YEAH, LET'S *NAIL* THE BITCH!

MOST RECENTLY, THE BROTHERHOOD OF THE FIST, A LOS ANGELES *NEO-NAZI GROUP*, DECLARED *WAR* ON LA MUSE FOR SOMETHING SHE SAID IN A TV INTERVIEW.

THE BROTHERHOOD IS ON THE *FBI WATCHLIST*. THEY DEAL IN DRUGS, WEAPONS-DEALING, HATE CRIMES, CONTRACT KILLINGS.

THEY TRIED TO KILL HER EARLIER *TODAY*.

I'VE INSTRUCTED MY MEN *NOT* TO INTERVENE WHEN THE BROTHERHOOD MAKES ITS MOVE AGAINST HER.

IT'LL BE *INTERESTING* TO SEE HOW SHE FARES AGAINST THEM.

Chapter 3:
RADICAL NEGOTIATION SKILLS

YOU KNOW I HAD MY PHONE TAPPED REGULARLY BACK WHEN I WAS A NOBODY ACTIVIST. YOU GET *USED* TO IT.

NOT *ME!* WIRE TAPS! AND *DEATH THREATS?!* I CAN'T *TAKE* THIS! I HAVE A NORMAL LIFE!

WHOOP. HOLD ON, THAT'S MY *PHONE*.

WHAT DO YOU *WANT*, TODD?

TODD! THAT LITTLE SHIT! DON'T AGREE TO ANYTHING! NOT EVEN *VERBALLY!*

I AM SO *FUCKED!*

I'M AT THE HEADQUARTERS OF THE BROTHERHOOD OF THE FIST!

THEY TOOK ME *HOSTAGE!*

IF YOU DON'T COME, THEY'LL *KILL* ME!

TODD, YOU'RE A SKINNY *GEEK*! WHAT WERE YOU THINKING, WALKING INTO A DEN OF NEO-NAZIS?

I WANTED TO PUT 'EM IN MY *DOCUMENTARY* ABOUT HOW PEOPLE FEEL ABOUT YOU!

NEO-NAZIS?!

I TOLD YOU TO *STOP* TRYING TO CASH IN ON ME!

PLEASE! PLEASE! IT'S YOU THEY WANT! NOT ME!

COME ALONE. START FLYING. WE'LL *TEXT* YOU THE PLACE WHERE MY MEN WILL PICK YOU UP.

DON'T HURT ME... I STILL HAVEN'T GOT A CAA AGENT... OR A FILM INTO SUNDANCE... *CLICK!*

WHAT'S GOING ON?

NO BIGGIE. I JUST GOTTA GO BAIL TODD OUT.

YOU GO WITH *TIM*, HAVE HIM KISS YOU AND LICK YOU ALL OVER. THINK "HAPPY", LIBBY. *HAPPY.*

SIGH.

41

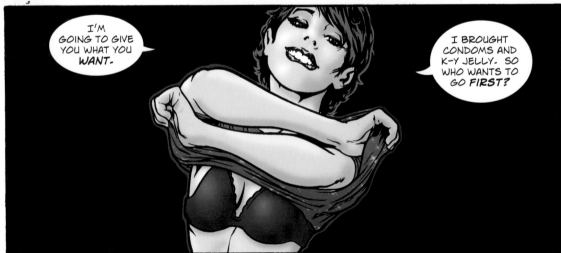

44

YOU **FUCKED** THEM?!!

NOT **ALL** OF 'EM.

IT WAS SORT OF AN **ORGY.** THEY FUCKED EACH OTHER TOO.

WHAT WERE YOU **THINKING?!**

I FIGURED IT WAS BETTER THAN **KILLING** THEM.

"IT WAS THE EASIEST WAY FOR ME TO **REWIRE** THEIR BRAINS. THE HATE, THE FEAR, AND THE ANGER WERE FUCKED RIGHT OUT OF THEM."

"I CURED AT LEAST TWO OF THEM OF HIV, ONE CASE OF CHLAMYDIA, AND IT WAS AMAZING HOW MANY OF 'EM HAD **HERPES.** I CURED THAT TOO."

"IT WAS KIND OF BEAUTIFUL. THEY WERE CRYING AND LAUGHING, IT WAS LIKE THEY WERE BEING CLEANSED."

"THEY'LL NEVER HURT ANYBODY EVER AGAIN."

"ALL IN ALL, I'D SAY IT WAS A **GOOD** NIGHT'S WORK."

AND **TODD** WAS THERE?

DON'T TELL ME HE FILMED IT!!

HE DID, BUT DON'T **WORRY.** HERE'S THE TAPE. I'M GUESSING YOU'LL WANT TO KEEP IT SOMEPLACE **SAFE.**

45

LIBBY, CALM DOWN—

SHE **RAPED** A ROOMFUL OF NEO-NAZIS! HOW DO I EVEN **BEGIN** TO PROCESS THAT?!

WELL, TECHNICALLY, WOMEN **CAN'T** RAPE MEN...

SHUT UP!

YOU KNOW, THIS GIVES ME AN IDEA. MAYBE THIS SHOULD BE MY NEXT CAMPAIGN: THE "FUCK FOR WORLD PEACE" TOUR.

NO!!

YOU'RE SUCH A PRUDE!

I'M **NOT** A PRUDE!

I'M GONNA BE SICK!

AT LEAST WE'RE IN THE CLEAR AND EVERYTHING'S OKAY...

YUP. G'NIGHT.

DUDE, LISTEN! I'M NOT KIDDING! I GOT THE **MOTHERLODE!**

GET READY TO FIRE UP YOUR **DVD** BURNERS!

A **LA MUSE SEX TAPE!** WE'RE TALKING NON-STOP GANGBANG!

NO, I HANDED HER A BLANK TAPE! I GOT THE **ORIGINAL** RIGHT HERE!

WE ARE GONNA BE **RICH!!**

SO YOU LIVE IN A STARVING VILLAGE IN ETHIOPIA, WITH NO HOPE OF **FOOD RELIEF** REACHING YOU IN TIME BECAUSE OF RED TAPE, AND YOU'RE JUST WAITING TO DIE.

ONE MORNING, YOU WAKE UP TO FIND THE LAND IS NO LONGER BARREN. THE SOIL IS **RICH** AND FERTILE.

MILLET CROPS AND TREES FILLED WITH FRUIT, THERE'S **MOISTURE** IN THE AIR AND CLOUDS TO ENSURE REGULAR RAINFALL.

THERE'S **CLEAN WATER** IN YOUR WELLS.

SUDDENLY, DESERTS ACROSS AFRICA ARE RICH WITH SOIL AND CROPS AND TREES AND FOOD. INCLUDING **NON-INDIGENOUS** FRUITS LIKE BANANAS AND ORANGES.

YOU MIGHT THINK IT WAS A *MIRACLE*, GOD FINALLY TOOK PITY AND DECIDED TO STEP IN AND END HUNGER.

YOU MIGHT BE RIGHT.

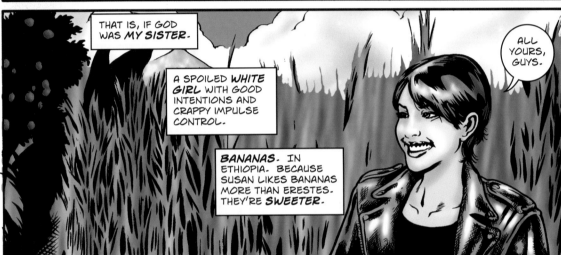

THAT IS, IF GOD WAS *MY SISTER*.

A SPOILED *WHITE GIRL* WITH GOOD INTENTIONS AND CRAPPY IMPULSE CONTROL.

BANANAS. IN ETHIOPIA. BECAUSE SUSAN LIKES BANANAS MORE THAN ERESTES. THEY'RE *SWEETER*.

ALL YOURS, GUYS.

AND YES, SHE *KNEW* ABOUT THE SOCIAL AND ECONOMIC UPHEAVAL THIS WAS GOING TO CAUSE, AND SHE WENT AHEAD WITH IT ANYWAY.

WITH NO CAMERAS AROUND, SO NO ONE CAN PROVE IT WAS *HER* THAT DID ALL THIS.

Chapter 4:
BECAUSE SHE LIKED BANANAS

AT THIS POINT, EVEN I DON'T KNOW *HOW* FAR SHE'S WILLING TO GO. ALL I CAN DO IS LIVE MY LIFE AND PRAY THINGS DON'T GO *BUGFUCK.*

'MORNING, JEFF. CAN YOU CALL MY SISTER AND CONFIRM OUR *MEETING* ABOUT HER DOCUMENTARY?

SHE'S HERE ALREADY, SHE'S WITH *DICK.*

WHAT?! WHERE ARE THEY?

HIS OFFICE FOR THE LAST TWENTY MINUTES.

NO NO NO NO NO...!

YEAH, YOU *LIKE* THAT, DON'T YOU, DICK! TELL ME YOU LIKE THAT!

OOOH YES! YES! MY GOD, YES!

SUSAN! WHAT DO YOU THINK YOU'RE ---

...DOING?

HEY, LIB. JUST RECONFIGURING DICK'S *SPINE* SO HIS BACK DOESN'T HURT.

I'VE ALSO OPENED UP HIS *CHAKRAS.*

AHHH---

49

WHAT DID YOU *THINK* I WAS DOING WITH HIM?

THESE DAYS, I THINK YOU'RE CAPABLE OF *ANYTHING.*

CHILL, LIBBY. I WAS JUST TALKING TO DICK ABOUT HIS WIFE SPONSORING ALTERNATE ENERGY VENTURES...

I WANTED TO *COVER* IT IN THE DOCUMENTARY...

LOOK, THIS IS WHERE I *WORK!* I DON'T WANT YOU SEXING UP OR MIND-BENDING MY BOSS OR MY COLLEAGUES—!

NOT EVEN TO MAKE DICK *NICER* TO YOU?

NO!

AAAAAAATTTTTTTTTTTAAAAAAAAAA!

DID TIME JUST *PAUSE?* WHAT THE HELL JUST HAPPENED?

SOMETHING WANTED TO COME THROUGH TO OUR UNIVERSE...

TRIED TO GROW A HUMAN BODY FROM SCRATCH AND *FAILED.*

IT'S *GONE* NOW.

WAS IT ONE OF **OUR** PEOPLE?

WHY DID IT WANT TO COME HERE?

YEAH.

I DUNNO, IF IT COMES BACK, I'LL **ASK**...

LIBBY! SUSAN!

TODD! WHAT ARE **YOU** DOING HERE?

I WAS MEETING **PETER CHU**. I THINK HE'S GONNA **SIGN** ME.

HEY, SUSAN, I'VE GOT A MOVIE I THINK YOU'D BE **PERFECT** FOR!

IT'S A **SUPERHEROINE** MOVIE--

I'M NOT AN **ACTRESS**, TODD.

NO, REALLY! IT'D BE A **BLOCKBUSTER!** YOU'LL FUCKIN' **KILL**, AND WE WON'T EVEN NEED SPECIAL EFFECTS BECAUSE YOU CAN --

TODD, WE'RE **TRYING** TO HAVE A MEETING HERE.

I CAN GIVE YOU THE SCREENPLAY --

GOODBYE, TODD!

BITCH!

WAYNE, IS THE **ONLINE STORE** UP YET?

OKAY, START UPLOADING THE **TEASER** CLIPS.

REPORTS ARE IN, SIR. ALL OF AFRICA IS *FERTILE* NOW. AND THERE'S MORE FOOD AND CROPS THAN EVEN *TROOPS* AND *WARLORDS* CAN SEIZE.

JESUS CHRIST! IT'S *HER!* WHAT ELSE COULD HAVE CAUSED THIS?

THE UN IS IN SESSION *ALL DAY* ABOUT THIS.

AT THE RATE SHE'S GOING, SHE'LL MAKE AFRICA AND THE THIRD WORLD TOTALLY *SELF-SUFFICIENT.* THE STOCK MARKET'S IN *CHAOS* TODAY.

ALRIGHT, STEP UP THE *DIGGING.* DOES LACKLEY IN LOS ANGELES HAVE ANYTHING?

I'LL *CHECK,* SIR.

BACK IN LOS ANGELES.

WHAT THE HELL IS THIS!

WHAT DOES IT *LOOK* LIKE? THIS WAS LAST WEEKEND!

LA MUSE IS *GAY!* YOU PUBLISH THIS, RUIN HER *IMAGE...*

GIVE ME A FUCKING *BREAK!*

SHE'S *BI!* SHE'S BEEN BI SINCE COLLEGE! I WAS THERE!

NOBODY GIVES A *SHIT* IF SHE MUFF-DIVES!

BUT—

SHE DID INTERVIEWS WITH *THREE* LESBIAN AND GAY MAGAZINES LAST WEEK! OR DID YOU *MISS* THAT?

CAN YOU KEEP IT *DOWN,* PLEASE...?

52

LOOK, *EVERY* CELEBRITY DOES LESBIAN CHIC THESE DAYS TO GET INTO THE PAPERS! WHAT ARE YOU, LIVING IN THE *1950S?*

SO SHE KISSED A BUNCH OF GIRLS! *BIG FUCKING DEAL!*

OKAY, *OKAY,* I'LL DO BETTER ...

YOU SAID YOU'D HAVE *REAL DIRT* TO GIVE ME!

MY EDITOR'S ON MY BACK! MY *REPUTATION'S* RIDING ON THIS!

MY PEOPLE ARE OUT THERE, WATCHING AND WAITING, *OKAY?*

"SHE'S SO RECKLESS SHE'S *BOUND* TO MAKE A MISTAKE SOONER OR LATER..."

ALLOW ME.

AND YOU'RE SUSAN. WE HAVE THE SAME *AGENT.*

THANKS. YOU'RE... *CHAD,* RIGHT?

DON'T BE *COY.* MY AGENT IS MY SISTER.

HEY, *GO SIS!*

53

RIGHT NOW, ABOUT THREE *PAPARAZZI* ACROSS THE STREET ARE SNAPPING OUR PICTURE. THEY'RE GONNA BE WORTH ABOUT *TWENTY GRAND* BY TONIGHT.

AHH, FUCKIN' VULTURES. PRICE OF *FAME*, GOTTA PAY THE PIPER.

I THINK THEIR PICTURES WOULD BE WORTH A LOT MORE IF WE WERE UP TO SOMETHING.

CLICK!

CLICK!

CLICK!

ARE YOU SUGGESTING WE *GET* UP TO SOMETHING?

DEPENDS. YOU GONNA LIVE UP TO YOUR *REPUTATION?*

OKAY, SUSAN, DO YOU WANNA, LIKE, *HANG OUT* SOMETIME?

THERE'S A PREMIERE FOR THE *HUMAN RIGHTS FILM FESTIVAL* TOMORROW NIGHT. WANNA GO?

YOU GOT IT.

IT'S A DATE! I'LL CALL YOU ABOUT THE MEET.

HEY, I DIDN'T GIVE YOU MY *NUMBER!*

I HAVE *EVERYBODY'S* NUMBER!

CALL LACKLEY. HE'S GONNA WANNA *KNOW* ABOUT THIS.

THIS COULD BE GOOD!

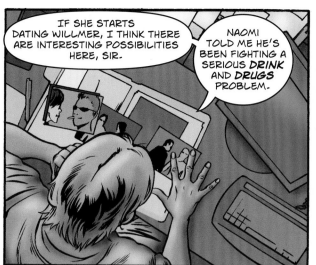

IF SHE STARTS DATING WILLMER, I THINK THERE ARE INTERESTING POSSIBILITIES HERE, SIR.

NAOMI TOLD ME HE'S BEEN FIGHTING A SERIOUS *DRINK* AND *DRUGS* PROBLEM.

INTERESTING. HAVE THAT VERIFIED, AGENT LACKLEY.

DIG UP *EVERYTHING* YOU CAN ON HIM. I HAVE AN IDEA...

Chapter 5:
THE CALM BEFORE THE MEDIA STORM

BRIXTON, LONDON.

8 HOURS AHEAD OF LOS ANGELES.

HELLO, STRANGER!

WELL WELL WELL... LOOK WHAT THE *CAT* DRAGGED IN!

I WAS WONDERIN' WHEN YOU WERE GONNA SHOW UP. *AFRICA'S* ALL OVER THE NEWS. AREN'T YOU AFRAID PEOPLE WILL *SEE* YOU?

NOPE.

NOBODY CAN SEE ME BUT *YOU*.

COME *HERE*, THEN!

AND YOU COME ALL THE WAY TO **LONDON** TO CONFESS ALL THAT TO ME? NO ONE'D **BELIEVE** ME IF I TELL ANYWAY.

I JUST WANTED TO **SEE** YOU, HON.

SOME SHIT'S GONNA HIT THE **FAN** AND IT COULD BE **A WHILE** BEFORE WE CAN MEET UP AGAIN.

OH, DON'T WORRY ABOUT ME. **SOCIAL WORK'S** NEVER DULL, EVEN AFTER YOU GOT RID OF VIOLENT CRIME IN BRITAIN.

HEY, I GOT AN IDEA. WHY DON'T YOU BECOME MY **PERSONAL ASSISTANT** AND KEEP ME HONEST?

NO CHANCE! I'LL GET **DRUNK** WITH YOU, I'LL EAT PUSSY WITH YOU, BUT I **WON'T** BE YOUR PERSONAL **MAGIC NEGRO!**

OH WELL, I HAD TO ASK.

YO, LIBBY. WHAT'S **UP?**

GET THE FUCK BACK HERE NOW!!

La Muse Sex Tape!

Order Now!

THE VIDEO ALLEGEDLY SHOWS *SUSAN LA MUSE* ENGAGED IN SEX WITH AT LEAST TWENTY NEO-NAZI SKINHEADS!

HOLEEEE SHIT! EVEN *I* COULDN'T MAKE THAT UP!

IT'S THE *HOTTEST* DOWNLOAD ON THE INTERNET RIGHT NOW, AND SALES OF THE DVD HAVE BEEN *HUGE!*

Chapter 6:
SEX, LIES, AND CREATIVE TRUTHS

SUSAN HERSELF IS SAID TO HAVE GONE INTO *HIDING,* AND SEVERAL PLANNED APPEARANCES HAVE BEEN CANCELLED!

THERE'S BEEN *NO WORD* FROM HER PUBLICIST!

MAYBE THIS IS THE BEGINNING OF THE *END,* SIR.

MAYBE, BUT LET'S NOT FORGET...

WE STILL HAVE TO FIND A WAY TO *KILL* HER.

WE ASKED SOME PEOPLE ON THE STREETS OF HOLLYWOOD WHAT *THEY* THOUGHT!

I DUNNO IF IT'S REALLY HER, BUT *SKINHEADS?*

THAT'S, LIKE, EEWWWWW!

I ORDERED THE DVD, SO I'M STILL *WAITING* TO SEE IT!

YO, CHAD! DUDE, IS THAT REALLY **YOU**?

YEAH, SORRY I HAVEN'T BEEN IN TOUCH, BUT MY **MANAGER** DIDN'T WANT ME TO BE SEEN WITH YOU, Y'KNOW?

YEAH, I KNOW THE SCORE.

YOU DOWNLOADED THE VIDEO, DIDN'T YOU?

HEH, YEAH. I DUNNO IF IT'S REALLY YOU, BUT THE IDEA OF YOU TAPPING A BUNCH OF BRUTAL, REPULSIVE SKINHEADS...

I THINK IT'S KINDA **HOT**.

MAYBE WHEN THIS IS OVER, WE CAN MEET UP. DUNNO IF IT CAN BE IN **PUBLIC**, BUT...

DUDE, I'LL CALL YOU. LATERS.

SO WHAT ARE WE GOING TO **DO** ABOUT THIS?

ONE: TOTAL **DENIAL**. SAY IT'S A LOOKALIKE.

AND WE CAN TRY SUING THESE GUYS FOR **DEFAMATION**. HOPE IT GOES AWAY.

TWO: COME CLEAN, BLAME IT ON DRUGS AND SAY YOU WERE **VICTIMIZED**.

PLAY UP THE **TRAUMA** OF RAPE, USE IT TO HIGHLIGHT THE PLIGHT OF RAPE VICTIMS.

PEOPLE WILL **STILL** HOLD IT AGAINST YOU.

THEY MIGHT THINK YOU'RE A **NEO-NAZI** AND YOU'RE ON A SHITLIST FOREVER.

YOU CAN MAKE A PUBLIC **APOLOGY**. WE CAN TRY TO BOOK YOU ON CHARITY GIGS, BUT I DON'T KNOW HOW MANY PEOPLE WILL WANT TO BE **SEEN** WITH YOU.

59

WELL, LIB? WHAT DO YOU *THINK*?

WHAT'S ON YOUR MIND, SUSAN?

YOU NEVER *WANTED* ME TO BECOME FAMOUS. HERE'S A CHANCE TO SHUT IT ALL DOWN.

I CAN LET THE MEDIA CRUCIFY ME AND *VANISH* INTO OBSCURITY, 'O THE HUMILIATION OF IT ALL!', 'THE PRICE OF FAME!' YADDA-YADDA-YADDA, NO ONE WILL *EVER* HEAR FROM ME AGAIN.

OR I CAN SPIN MY WAY *OUT* OF THIS.

"DICK HOOKED SUSAN UP WITH HOWARD "BEAR" THACKER, THE MOST **FEARED** ATTORNEY IN TOWN, AND HE IMMEDIATELY SERVED TODD'S PRODUCTION COMPANY WITH A **CEASE-AND-DESIST ORDER** ON THE TAPE."

"NO, I **WASN'T** AT THE MEETING WITH TODD AND HIS FRATBOY ASSHOLE PARTNERS STEVE AND CHUCK. I DIDN'T **NEED** TO WATCH THE BEAR EAT THEM ALIVE. I HAD WORK TO DO."

I DON'T **NEED** A LAWYER! I'M IN THE **RIGHT!**

THAT VIDEO IS **MY PROPERTY!** WE'VE ALREADY GOTTEN CLOSE TO A **MILLION DOLLARS** IN ORDERS!

YOU **NEVER** TOOK ME SERIOUSLY!

YOU ALWAYS **SNEERED** BECAUSE I WANTED TO BE FAMOUS!

YOU NEVER EVEN **WANTED** TO BE FAMOUS!

IT'S NOT FAIR!

IF IT WEREN'T FOR ME, YOU'D STILL BE A **NOBODY** COLLECTING PETITIONS! YOU COULDA STARRED IN MY PROJECTS, INTRODUCED ME TO YOUR AGENCY AND YOUR NEW A-LIST FRIENDS, BUT **NOOOO!**

YOU **OWED** ME! AND THIS IS PAYBACK!

HOW DO YOU LIKE KARMA **NOW?** HUH? I SHOT THE VIDEO, AND I OWN IT! AND THERE'S **NOTHING** YOU CAN DO ABOUT IT!

TWO WORDS, TODD.

RELEASE FORM.

OHHHH--- **SHIT.**

DID MS. LA MUSE SIGN A **RELEASE** ALLOWING YOU TO USE HER IMAGE AND LIKENESS?

I DIDN'T— I THOUGHT— I-I-

YOU *DIDN'T* —?!

WE THOUGHT YOU *TOOK CARE* OF THAT!

WELL, GENTLEMEN, YOU'VE JUST *ADMITTED* TO UNLAWFULLY USING HER IMAGE FOR PROFIT WITHOUT HER CONSENT, IN A MANNER DAMAGING TO HER REPUTATION AND EMOTIONAL WELL-BEING.

STUPID MOTHERFUCKER! I'LL KILL YOU!

YOU SCREWED US!

GENTLEMEN, YOU CAN STRANGLE HIM ON YOUR *OWN TIME.* WE WANT TO CONCLUDE OUR BUSINESS TODAY.

WHAT ARE YOUR *TERMS?*

STOP SELLING THE DVDS IMMEDIATELY, AND DONATE *ALL* PROCEEDS FROM SALES TO THIS LIST OF CHARITIES...

SHELTERS FOR BATTERED WOMEN, RAPE CRISIS CENTERS, WOMEN'S HEALTH CLINICS...

AND YOU SELL THE COMPANY AND FILMMAKING EQUIPMENT TO MS. LA MUSE FOR THE SUM OF *ONE DOLLAR.* YOU MAY REMAIN AS *EMPLOYEES* AT HER DISCRETION.

WHAT?!

I ALWAYS *WANTED* A PRODUCTION COMPANY. YOU JUST SAVED ME THE TROUBLE OF SETTING ONE UP.

THE DEVIL... YOU'RE THE DEVIL...

AND NOW I'M YOUR *BOSS.*

DON'T YOU JUST LOVE *KARMA?*

SIR, WE TRACKED SOME PEOPLE WHO ORDERED THE DVD. THEIR FAMILIES REPORTED THAT THEY HAD SOME KIND OF *PERSONALITY CHANGE!*

GET A HOLD OF A COPY AND HAVE OUR PEOPLE ANALYZE IT!

SO, SUSAN, CAN YOU TELL US *EXACTLY* WHAT HAPPENED?

THEY HAD MY FRIEND *HOSTAGE* AND THEY SAID THEY WERE GOING TO *KILL* HIM IF I DIDN'T SHOW UP. THEY HAD GUNS AND KNIVES, AND I WAS ON MY OWN.

THAT WAS INCREDIBLY *BRAVE* OF YOU...

I *WASN'T* RAPED. I MADE A *CHOICE.* I WANTED TO KEEP ANYONE FROM GETTING HURT. SO I KEPT THEM TALKING, AND THEN...

IT'S ALL RIGHT, SUSAN...

IF YOU CHECK WITH THE POLICE AND *FBI,* YOU'LL FIND THAT THE MORNING AFTER I HAD SEX WITH THEM, THOSE MEN ALL TURNED THEMSELVES IN.

THEY *AGREED* TO DO THAT.

SHE, LIKE, PUT OUT TO SAVE HER FRIEND? WOW!

THAT'S, LIKE, *WOW!*

NOW SHE'S A HERO AGAIN! *FUCK!*

64

ALL IN *ALL*, IT'S BEEN A PRETTY GOOD WEEK, DON'T YOU THINK?

ALMOST *TOO* GOOD.

AND I NOTICE YOU WERE NEVER *TOO* WORKED UP ABOUT THE TAPE GETTING OUT THERE.

OH, IT WAS SOMETHING I WANTED TO *TRY OUT*...

"I JUST ENCODED THE FOOTAGE WITH SOME SIGNALS FOR REJIGGING THE *ALPHA WAVES* IN THE BRAIN, RELEASING MORE ENDORPHINS, OPENING UP THEIR SYNAPSES, AND MAKING THEM MORE *AWARE*."

"AND THIS IS *EVERY* COPY?"

"YUP."

OOOH--- AHHH---!

OH GOD---!

YOU *KNEW* TODD WOULD RELEASE THE FOOTAGE? DID YOU *PLAN* ALL THIS?

I TRUSTED TODD TO BE *TODD*.

BRADLEY!

WHAT'S GOING ON!

65

THE WHOLE ANALYSIS TEAM IS **RESIGNING!** THEY JUST WATCHED THE **DISC** AND---

WE CAN'T WORK FOR YOU IN **GOOD CONSCIENCE** ANYMORE, SIR!

STOP PLAYING THE DVD! NOBODY ELSE WATCH IT! THAT'S AN ORDER!

OHH---! AHH---! OH GOD---!

YOU BETTER **NOT** BE MIND-CONTROLLING PEOPLE.

I JUST OPEN UP THEIR MINDS AND LET 'EM MAKE THEIR **OWN** DECISIONS, LIB.

NOW DO YOU SEE HOW **DANGEROUS** SHE IS?

DO YOU **SEE?**

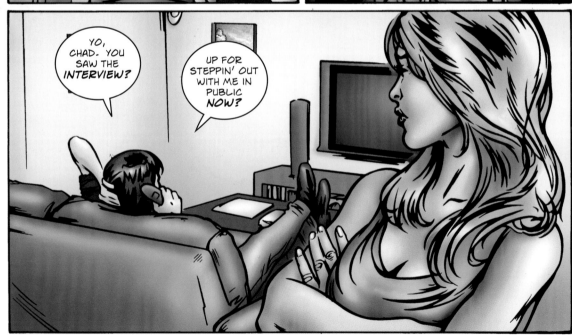

YO, CHAD. YOU SAW THE **INTERVIEW?**

UP FOR STEPPIN' OUT WITH ME IN PUBLIC **NOW?**

68

SO *CHAD WILMER'S* NEW MOVIE IS PREMIERING WITH GREAT BUZZ, AND I'VE NEGOTIATED AN *$11 MILLION DEAL* FOR HIS NEXT PROJECT. I'VE NEGOTIATED *THREE* PRODUCT SPONSORSHIP DEALS FOR SUSAN, AND EVEN WITH MOST OF HER FEE GOING TO CHARITY, THE REST IS IN *SEVEN FIGURES.*

I'M MAKING MORE MONEY THAN EVER, MY BOSS LOVES ME, AND *I'M MORE MISERABLE THAN EVER.*

Chapter 7:
LIFESTYLES OF THE NC-17

NATURALLY, CHAD ASKED SUSAN OUT TO HIS PREMIERE.

NOW THAT THE SEX TAPE SCANDAL'S *BLOWN OVER,* SUSAN AND CHAD HAVE OFFICIALLY STARTED DATING.

PEOPLE MAGAZINE CALLED THEM THE *NEW POWER COUPLE.*

HEY, *LA MUSE!* SO WHO ARE YOU GONNA BANG NEXT? THE *KU KLUX KLAN?*

I'LL CHECK MY DIARY!

COCKSUCKERS! I OUGHTTA...

AHH, CHILL. IT'S ALL *GOOD.*

AND ALL THE VULTURES AND PREDATORS WERE STILL GATHERING AROUND HER.

SIR, WE'VE CONFIRMED THAT CHAD WILMER STILL BUYS *NARCOTICS* FROM A SPECIFIC DEALER.

MARIJUANA, ECSTASY, GHB, AND OCCASIONALLY, HEROIN.

FIND OUT HOW *OFTEN* WILMER BUYS FROM HIM, WHEN AND HOW MUCH.

LET'S COOK UP SOMETHING *SPECIAL* FOR OUR MOVIE STAR.

EVERYTHING COMES *EASY* TO HER! THIS IS WHY SHE HAS TO BE *STOPPED!*

ACTUALLY, MY PEOPLE THINK THERE ARE *BIGGER* REASONS FOR HER TO BE STOPPED...

NAOMI PINNEY!

OH MY GOD!

S-SUSAN! HI...!

HOW *ARE* YOU, GIRL? I'VE BEEN *THINKING* ABOUT YOU!

DID YOU EVER WRITE YOUR NOVEL?

I'VE BEEN WAITING *YEARS* TO READ IT!

SO ARE YOU MOSTLY LIVIN' THE *FREELANCE* LIFE THESE DAYS?

YEAH, WELL, YOU KNOW...

SAY, WOULD IT HELP YOU TO HAVE AN *INTERVIEW* WITH ME?

IT'D BE A *SCOOP* FOR YOU, RIGHT?

ER, YEAH, BUT... ARE YOU *SURE?*

CALL *TIM* AT RASKIN! HE WON'T BLOW YOU OFF!

YOU KNOW INTERVIEWS, I JUST PLAY A *SIMULACRA* OF WHATEVER MY SELF. I'M ALL ABOUT THE SIMULACRA, BABY!

"SIMULACRA"--- *BITCH!* BRINGING UP BAUDRILLARD TO ME...! *I* WAS THE ONE WHO GOT HER TO READ HIM!

DOESN'T PINNEY *HATE* YOU...?

ALL THE *MORE* REASON TO HAVE HER *CLOSE.*

HEY, LA MUSE! YOU GAY OR STRAIGHT? GET OFF THE FENCE!

THERE IS NO FENCE, BABY!

WHEN THEY'RE NOT ARGUING WITH YOU, THEY'RE *HITTING* ON YOU. I DON'T GET WHY NOBODY'S HIT ON *ME*.

LIB, YOU GIVE OFF SUCH A SERIOUSLY "UPTIGHT AND STRAIGHT" VIBE, THEY CAN *SMELL* IT OFF YOU.

EAT SHIT AND DIE!

WHERE'S *TIM* ANYWAY?

WE HAD A *FIGHT* THE OTHER NIGHT AND WE HAVEN'T REALLY TALKED...

OH, I CAN *PINPOINT* HIM IF YOU WANT...

DON'T *WORRY* ABOUT IT. I'LL SEE HIM LATER...

YOU *LIVE* IN LA, YOU WORK IN THE MEDIA, AND YOU'RE *IN THE CLOSET!* HOW IRONIC IS THAT!

MY FAMILY IN WISCONSIN IS *REALLY* RELIGIOUS!

BUT IT'S NO BIG DEAL... LIBBY AND I HAVE AN *OPEN* RELATIONSHIP.

REALLY? DOES *SHE* KNOW THAT?

ER... NO.

SO WHAT ARE YOU GONNA *DO?*

NOTHING. IT'S NONE OF MY BUSINESS.

AND I *WON'T* TELL HER.

BUT *YOU'RE* GOING TO BREAK UP WITH HER.

BUT—

TIM, YOU LIKE *COCK,* NOT *BOOBS.* DO YOURSELF A FAVOR. COME OUT AND END IT.

THAT WAY, I WON'T HAVE TO DO SOMETHING *DISGUSTING* TO YOU FOR CHEATING ON MY SISTER.

TIM, MY GREAT WHITE HOPE, MY BLUE-EYED BOY, IT'S BEEN A **WHILE** SINCE WE HAD OUR LITTLE TALKS.

AHH, I'M **GOOD**, MIRIAM. IT'S ALL GOOD...

IS YOUR **BREAK-UP** GOING TO AFFECT YOUR RELATIONSHIP WITH SUSAN?

YOU HEARD?

AH. WELL, IT WAS **SUSAN** WHO MADE ME BREAK UP WITH LIBBY OR SHE WOULD'VE FIRED ME. THAT'S FOR STARTERS.

WELL, I WANT YOU TO STICK **CLOSE** TO HER FROM NOW ON. A LOT OF LITTLE BIRDIES TELL ME PEOPLE ARE **STILL** GUNNING FOR HER.

BUT SHE **ALREADY** WEATHERED THE SEX TAPE. SHE'S **OUT** ABOUT BEING BI. WHAT COULD **POSSIBLY** HURT HER NOW?

THINK, TIM! SHE'S DATING **CHAD**, WHO'S ALSO OUR CLIENT! AND HE'S GOT A LOT **MORE** TO HIDE THAN SHE DOES!

THE TWO OF THEM TOGETHER IS LIKE A LIT **MATCH** AND A **POWDER KEG**! IT'S YOUR JOB TO KEEP THEM FROM IGNITING IN PUBLIC!

YEAH, BUT –

PUBLIC RELATIONS IS A **COLD WAR**, TIM.

ARE YOU GOING TO BE A **GOOD SOLDIER** OR DO I HAVE TO GET SOMEONE ELSE?

75

YO, LIB. OUR GUY TRIED TO ENTER THIS UNIVERSE BY BECOMING A MASS OF *DARK MATTER.*

DID HE COME THROUGH?

NOPE.

HE MESSED UP AN ENTIRE *GALAXY,* BLEW CHUNKS OF DARK MATTER ALL OVER THE PLACE. NEARLY SHREDDED THE *UNIVERSE.*

SUSAN—

HOLD ON! I'M JUST REPAIRING SOME DARK FABRIC.

THERE! ALL DONE!

I GOT A CALL FROM *CHAD'S* MANAGER.

SHE APOLOGIZED FOR CHAD SKIPPING OUT ON GOING TO THE GAY PRIDE PARADE WITH YOU.

I FIGURED HE WOULD. HIS MANAGER DOESN'T WANT HIM TO GET *TOO CLOSELY* ASSOCIATED, MIGHT AFFECT HIS STANDING AS THE NEXT BIG *ACTION STAR.*

"GAY-FRIENDLY, BUT NOT *TOO* FRIENDLY". IT'S HILARIOUS!

GLAD YOU'RE TAKING IT WELL.

AHH, IT'S NOT LIKE MY THING WITH CHAD IS GONNA *LAST.*

DOES HE *KNOW* HE'S YOUR BEARD?

WELL -- *WHOA!*

ALLL-RIGHT, IT'S *KARMABANQUE RADIO*, AND WE HAVE A SPECIAL GUEST ON THE LINE, OUR FRIEND *SUSAN LA MUSE*!

HEYY, MAX, HEY, STACY!

SO SUSAN HAS BEEN FIGHTING THE *GOOD FIGHT* AGAINST THE CORPORATE OCCUPIERS AND ENVIRONMENTAL HOLOCAUST DENIERS! SHE JUST HELPED DRIVE *COKE* OUT OF BHOPAL!

YUP! NO COKE FACTORIES *STEALING* THE PEOPLE'S DRINKING WATER TO MAKE SODA!

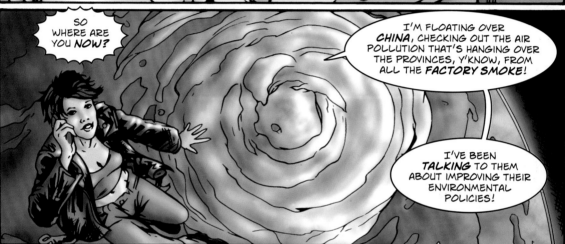

SO WHERE ARE YOU *NOW?*

I'M FLOATING OVER *CHINA*, CHECKING OUT THE AIR POLLUTION THAT'S HANGING OVER THE PROVINCES, Y'KNOW, FROM ALL THE *FACTORY SMOKE*!

I'VE BEEN *TALKING* TO THEM ABOUT IMPROVING THEIR ENVIRONMENTAL POLICIES!

SIR, WE HAVE REAL-TIME *SATELLITE PHOTOS* THAT SHOW THE POLLUTION OVER CHINA AND SOUTHEAST ASIA DISSOLVING INTO CLEAN AIR!

SHE WAS DOING *MORE* THAN JUST "CHECKING OUT"!

AND YOU'VE BEEN PRETTY *VOCAL* ABOUT THE BANKS ENCOURAGING *ENVIRONMENTALLY UNSOUND* BUSINESS PRACTICES...

YEAH, AND SEIZING PEOPLE'S *ASSETS* AND *HOMES*, AND PUTTING OUR MONEY INTO STUFF THAT'S MESSING UP THE ENVIRONMENT!

ANOTHER THING I'M INTO IS *MICROFINANCING*! YOU KNOW, SETTING UP LOANS FOR PEOPLE IN THE THIRD WORLD TO BUY ASSETS THAT THEY NEED TO MAKE A LIVING WITH.

ORGANIZATIONS LIKE *KIVA-ORG* ARE GOOD FOR THAT.

FOR JUST **25 BUCKS**, YOU CAN HELP A SINGLE MOTHER IN KENYA BUY A **SEWING MACHINE** TO TAILOR CLOTHES TO EARN MONEY AND FEED HER KIDS, AND SHE'LL PAY YOU BACK!

AND YOU TAKE THAT 25 BUCKS AND LOAN IT TO **ANOTHER** PERSON IN, LIKE, BENIN!

WE BLOW 25 BUCKS EASY ON LATTES AND **BOOZE**! WHY NOT USE IT TO DO SOMETHING **CONSTRUCTIVE** INSTEAD?

THIS HIPPY-TRIPPY **BULLSHIT** IS JUST COVER FOR HER **REAL** AGENDA!

SIR, THE **DRUGS** HAVE BEEN DELIVERED TO THE DEALER, AND THE HIT TEAMS ARE STANDING BY.

GOOD!

SO **WHAT** IF SHE'S CAN FLY AND SAVE THE WORLD?

YOU'RE THE BIGGEST **MOVIE STAR** IN THE WORLD, MAN!

$100 MILLION OPENING WEEKEND!

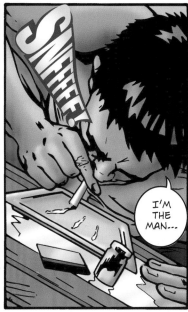

Chapter 8: BIG DATE, BAD DRUGS

CHAD WILMER HAS A HISTORY OF DRUG AND ALCOHOL ABUSE, STEMMING FROM *DEEP INSECURITY* AND LOW SELF-ESTEEM THAT HE KEEPS WELL-HIDDEN.

HE HAS BEEN IN *REHAB* ONCE AND THAT WAS KEPT QUIET.

MY SOURCE SAID HE HAS BEGUN USING DRUGS *AGAIN*, AS RELIEF FROM THE PRESSURES OF *STARDOM* AND HIS NEW RELATIONSHIP WITH THE TARGET!

WE'RE GOING TO USE THAT *AGAINST* HER!

YOU KNOW, SUSAN, I HAVE *NO IDEA* WHAT KIND OF WORLD YOU'RE GOING TO CREATE, AND THAT SCARES ME!

COME ON! YOU'RE BRINGING THIS UP TO AVOID TALKING ABOUT NOT GETTING *LAID*!

GO ON, GET BACK IN THE SADDLE! THERE'S *PLENTY* OF MAN-FLESH TO CHOOSE FROM HERE!

THEY'RE ALL EITHER AIRHEADS OR SNAKES OR *BOTH*!

YOU'RE NOT SUPPOSED TO *MARRY* ONE, JUST BONK ONE!

CAN YOU *NOT* SAY THIS IN FRONT OF CHAD? HE'S MY *CLIENT*! I DON'T WANT HIM TO GET ANY IDEAS ABOUT ME!

OH, HE DOESN'T CARE! HE'S TOO INTO *HIMSELF* TO LISTEN TO US!

OKAY, CHAD AND I ARE GONNA GET SOME *PRIVATE TIME* IN HIS SUITE!

GO FORTH AND *CONQUER,* GIRL! HAVE FUN!

RIGHT! WE'LL *SEE* ABOUT NOT GETTING LAID!

WE HAVE ARRANGED FOR WILMER'S HEROIN TO BE OF A *HIGHER CONCENTRATION,* WHICH WOULD LIKELY BE *LETHAL* TO HIM.

IF HE DIES, THE *TARGET* WILL BE EMBROILED IN THE SCANDAL, WHICH WILL TAINT HER *REPUTATION!*

I HAVE A **REAL BAD** FEELING TONIGHT... I SAW CHAD'S **DEALER** HOOKING HIM UP EARLIER ...

WHY ARE YOU SO **WORKED UP**, TIM? DID MARIAM GIVE YOU THE **STINK-EYE?**

DAMN STRAIGHT! I WAS LUCKY SHE DIDN'T **FIRE** ME FOR NOT CATCHING THE **SEX TAPE** BEFORE IT HIT!

I DON'T WANT **ANOTHER** SHIT-STORM ON MY WATCH!

AHHH, YOU DON'T NEED TO WORRY ABOUT SUSAN! SHE'S A LAW UNTO **HERSELF!**

ER, LIBBY, SHOULD YOU BE KNOCKING BACK THE **BOOZE** LIKE THAT?

WHY NOT! IT'S ABOUT **TIME** I LET MY HAIR DOWN!

WHY SHOULD **I** BE THE RESPONSIBLE ONE ALL THE TIME?

AND YOU DON'T HAVE TO WORRY ABOUT SUSAN DOING DRUGS! SHE DOESN'T **NEED** TO! SHE'S HER OWN **CONTACT HIGH!** SHE CAN CREATE ANY HIGH OR ALTERED STATE IN HERSELF JUST BY **THINKING** IT! SHE CAN CHANGE HER **HAIR COLOR** JUST BY THINKING IT! NO NEED FOR **TOXIC CHEMICALS** OR BLEACHES!

BECAUSE SHE'S AN **ALIEN!** SHE DOESN'T **HAVE** TO LIVE BY HUMAN RULES!

REALLY?

THAT'S VERY INTERESTING.

TELL ME **MORE.**

WITH SO MANY PEOPLE THERE TONIGHT, THERE IS NO WAY *THIS* SCANDAL WON'T STICK TO THE TARGET.

THEN THERE'S THE *OTHER* FRONT WE'RE ATTACKING HER FROM.

WE PICKED HER FORMER THESIS ADVISOR, HER INUIT FRIEND, A BRAZILIAN RAIN FOREST ACTIVIST, HER LOVER IN LONDON, HER ELEMENTARY SCHOOL TEACHER, ANOTHER CHILDHOOD FRIEND --

-- AND WE'VE TARGETED THEM FOR *LIQUIDATION!*

THE HITS WILL LOOK LIKE RANDOM CRIMES, ROBBERIES, AND SO ON, BUT IT WILL SEND A *MESSAGE* TO HER:

WE CAN TOUCH ANY OF HER LOVED ONES ANYTIME!

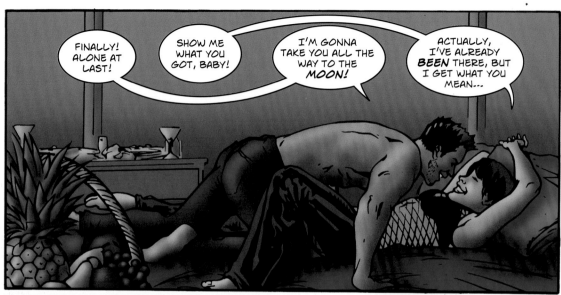

SUSAN!

SIGH!

BITCH!

HAVE ANY OF THE *HIT TEAMS* REPORTED IN YET?

NO, SIR.

"SHE *COULDN'T* HAVE GOT THERE IN TIME. COULD SHE?"

SIR?

KEEP TRYING! TELL ME THE *MINUTE* YOU HEAR ANYTHING!

GOOD THING I GOT AN *EXTRA KEY* FOR EMERGENCIES...

TIM, THEY'RE PROBABLY BOFFING THEIR BRAINS OUT! THEY'LL BE *PISSED* WHEN WE BARGE IN!

SO I'LL *APOLOGIZE* AND WE LEAVE!

OH FUCK!

I TOOK AWAY YOUR SUSCEPTIBILITY TO GETTING MURDERED! WAS THAT **WRONG** OF ME?

I **ACCEPTED** THAT PEOPLE MIGHT ATTACK YOU THROUGH ME, BUT YOU COULD'VE BLOODY TOLD ME ABOUT THIS— THIS **WHAMMY FIELD!**

WELL, I DIDN'T THINK I'D **HAVE** TO! I'M **SORRY!**

YOU'RE INJECTING HIM WITH **SALT?**

FINGERS CROSSED!

BACK IN COLLEGE, I KNEW A **DRUMMER** WHO OD'D, AND... ANYWAY, LONG STORY!

HOW DO YOU EVEN **KNOW** HOW TO DO THIS?

I DON'T FUCKING **BELIEVE** THIS!

LOOK, BABE, I GOTTA CHECK ON EVERYONE **ELSE** I KNOW!

I'LL CALL YOU **LATER,** OKAY?

NONE OF THE TEAMS HAVE PHONED IN... IT **HAS** TO BE HER! HOW...?

SIR, CODENAME: **CASANOVA** IS ON THE LINE!

I HOPE YOU HAVE **GOOD NEWS!**

SIR! I GOT HER **SISTER** TO TALK! I'VE GOT IT! **THE KEY!**

SHE'S AN **ALIEN!** AND HER POWERS ARE BASED ON **THOUGHT!**

IF WE CAN STOP HER FROM BEING ABLE TO **THINK**—

YOU JUST GAVE US THE KEY TO **STOPPING** HER!

GET AN **ASSAULT TEAM** READY!

YOU RAN OFF AND LEFT ME TO CLEAN UP YOUR *MESS!*

AGAIN!

I HAVE *HAD IT* WITH YOU!

I HAD TO MAKE SURE MY POLITICAL SCIENCE PROFESSOR WAS *OKAY!*

THEY TRIED TO HIT *MARTINE* IN LONDON AND *AMORAK* UP NORTH!

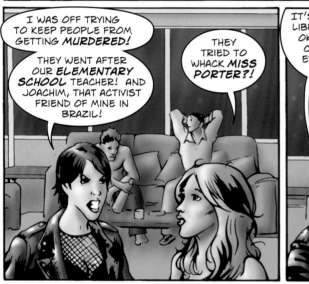

I WAS OFF TRYING TO KEEP PEOPLE FROM GETTING *MURDERED!*

THEY WENT AFTER OUR *ELEMENTARY SCHOOL* TEACHER! AND JOACHIM, THAT ACTIVIST FRIEND OF MINE IN BRAZIL!

THEY TRIED TO WHACK *MISS PORTER?!*

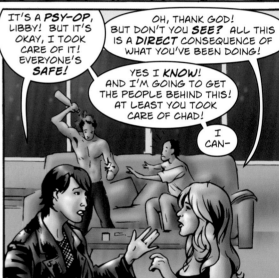

IT'S A *PSY-OP,* LIBBY! BUT IT'S OKAY, I TOOK CARE OF IT! EVERYONE'S *SAFE!*

OH, THANK GOD! BUT DON'T YOU *SEE?* ALL THIS IS A *DIRECT* CONSEQUENCE OF WHAT YOU'VE BEEN DOING!

YES I *KNOW!* AND I'M GOING TO GET THE PEOPLE BEHIND THIS! AT LEAST YOU TOOK CARE OF CHAD!

I CAN—

AAAAAAUUUUUUUUUUH!

WHOA!

OH MY GOD!

EEEYYYYAAAAAAAAAAAH!

DAMN, MOVIES STARS ARE MESSED UP!

94

SUSAN, HOW MUCH **LONGER?** TIM CAN'T KEEP THE PRESS BACK ANY LONGER!

QUIET! I'M RE-GROWING HIS LUNGS!

AND REWIRING HIS BRAIN. I SHOULD'VE DONE IT **WEEKS** AGO...

HERE HE S! GOOD AS NEW!

SO, CHAD, WHAT **WAS** THAT IMMOLATION-DEFENESTRATION STUNT ABOUT?

JUST ONE LAST **JACKASS** HURRAH! MAN, WAS I DUMB! I'M NEVER DOING THAT KIND OF THING **AGAIN!**

YOU'RE A **BAD BOY,** CHAD! TELL US MORE!

STRAIGHT UP!

WELL, THAT DIDN'T GO **TOO** BADLY...

JUST STAY AWAY FROM ME! I NEED TO **PROCESS** ALL THIS! YOU CAN FLY HOME YOURSELF, OKAY?

SIGH! POOR LIBBY...

SUSAN LA MUSE! HALT!

PUT YOUR HANDS BEHIND YOUR HEAD!

YOU ARE UNDER ARREST!

BZZZZZZZZZZZZ!

GROAN---!

KABC WITH YOUR MORNING COMMUTE! IT'S A **BEAUTIFUL** MORNING IN LA, WITH TEMPERATURES IN THE LOW-70S AND HUMIDITY AT 30%! TRAFFIC ON THE 101 FREEWAY IS...

'MORNING, JASON. **MESSAGES?**

CHRIS COLWELL WANTS TO KNOW IF YOU'VE READ HIS SCRIPT. RICK CALLED FROM PARAMOUNT. LORENZO WANTED TO CONFIRM LUNCH. AND HARVEY WANTS AN ANSWER BY 3PM.

CALL LORENZO AND TELL HIM WE'RE STILL ON. LET HARVEY STEW TILL 3.

HI, TIM. WHAT'S UP?

HAVE YOU HEARD FROM **SUSAN?**

NOT SINCE I LEFT HER AT THE PARTY LAST NIGHT.

SHE HASN'T CALLED ME EITHER! IT'S NOT **LIKE** HER TO GO QUIET LIKE THIS!

I WOULDN'T WORRY. SHE'S PROBABLY OFF MAPPING THE GENOME OF **EBOLA** OR SOMETHING.

SHE ALREADY DID THAT **LAST** WEEK!

OH YEAH, THAT'S RIGHT! LOOK, SHE'LL TURN UP!

Chapter 9: *A VERY EXTRAORDINARY RENDITION*

THERE'S **NOTHING** TO SHOW HOW SHE COULD HAVE PULLED OFF ANY OF HER STUNTS!

SHE'S AN **ALIEN!** SHE **CAN'T** BE HUMAN!

WALK ME THROUGH THE **TAKEDOWN** AGAIN!

WELL, ARMED UNITS SURROUNDED HER ON A STREET LAST NIGHT AND ORDERED HER TO **SURRENDER.**

THEY ALSO TURNED ON THE **SONIC EMITTER.**

'THE TARGET COLLAPSED.

'SHE REMAINED UNCONSCIOUS WHEN THEY BROUGHT HER IN AND STRAPPED HER TO THE CHAIR.'

SHE ONLY WOKE UP SHORTLY AFTER YOU ARRIVED THIS MORNING.

WHO'S CONDUCTING THE INTERROGATION?

'AGENT KENTON, SIR.'

'GOOD. HE'S GOOD. NO NEED TO BE SOFT WITH HER. I WANT HER **BROKEN.'**

OOOKAAYY...

I'M NOT REALLY **INTO** BONDAGE, BUT HEY, 'TRY ANYTHING ONCE EXCEPT INCEST AND MORRIS DANCING', **RIGHT?**

WHAT'S THAT **BUZZING** IN THE AIR?

THAT IS A HYPERSONIC EMITTER. IT'S WHAT'S **STOPPING** YOU FROM BEING ABLE TO CONCENTRATE AND USE YOUR **POWERS**.

DO YOU KNOW **WHY** YOU'RE HERE?

YOU WANT ME TO ENDORSE SOME **TORTURE** PRODUCTS?

YOU'RE IN A **LOT** OF TROUBLE. YOUR CIVIL RIGHTS DON'T APPLY. FORGET HABEUS CORPUS.

YEAH, YEAH, I GET IT. DUE PROCESS DOESN'T LIVE HERE.

I WANT TO KNOW WHERE YOUR **POWERS** COME FROM, WHO OR WHAT YOU REALLY **ARE**, ARE THERE ANY **MORE** LIKE YOU, AND I WANT THE **TRUTH!**

NONE OF THAT SPIN-DOCTORED **BULLSHIT** YOU'VE BEEN FEEDING THE MEDIA!

YOU DON'T BELIEVE **PEOPLE MAGAZINE?** SHAME ON YOU!

YOU **THINK** THIS IS A JOKE?

YOU WANT TO BE WATERBOARDED? *RAPED?*

WE CAN MAKE YOU DISAPPEAR! NONE OF YOUR FRIENDS AND FAMILY WILL *EVER* KNOW WHAT HAPPENED TO YOU! YOU'LL JUST BE ANOTHER *UNSOLVED MYSTERY!* A WASTE OF LIFE AND POTENTIAL!

IS THAT WHAT YOU WANT?

I HAVE A *CONFESSION* TO MAKE.

YES?

I'M NOT *JEWISH.*

I KNOW, SOMETIMES I *TALK* LIKE A JEWISH GIRL. COMES FROM LIVING IN *NEW YORK.* SORRY.

GEE. I'M SENSING A LOT OF *HOSTILITY* IN YOU.

MAN, WHAT KIND OF **VETTING** PROCESS DO YOU HAVE HERE ANYWAY? ALL YOUR GUYS HERE HAVE **SERIOUS ISSUES!**

IT'S EITHER A DADDY THING, OR A MOMMY THING, OR A SHAME THING, OR A GUILT THING! A SHRINK WOULD MAKE A **FORTUNE** OFF 'EM!

I MEAN, OKAY, I GET IT, YOU **NEED** TO BE AN ASSHOLE TO DO THE KINDS OF THINGS YOU DO HERE, BUT STILL...

ARE YOU **FINISHED?**

HEY, HOW YA DOIN'? NICE TO **MEET** YOU FINALLY!

CUTE TRICK, BREAKING MY MEN DOWN! AND THEY'VE BEEN TRAINED TO **WITHSTAND** INTERROGATION!

I DIDN'T INTERROGATE THEM. I JUST **TALKED** TO THEM AND EVERYTHING CAME POURING OUT.

I MEAN, TAKE **YOU,** FOR INSTANCE! IVY LEAGUE, **SKULL-&-BONES,** TRAINED DEATH SQUADS IN EL SALVADOR, YOUR WIFE DOESN'T UNDERSTAND YOU...

MS. LA MUSE, I'LL CUT TO THE **CHASE.**

IF YOU WANT TO LIVE, YOU COME WORK FOR **US!**

YOU'VE CAUSED **MASSIVE CHAOS** IN THE STOCK MARKET AND THE ECONOMY.

IT'S NOT **MY FAULT** THE THIRD WORLD DECIDED TO DEFAULT ON THEIR DEBTS.

YOU **ENABLED** THEM.

IMAGINE THE **GOOD** YOU COULD DO IF YOU WERE ON **OUR** SIDE.

LIKE WHAT? KEEP THE WORLD DEPENDENT ON OIL? FIGHT **WARS** YOU WANT TO WIN?

HELP YOUR BOSSES **RAPE** THE PLANET AND LINE THEIR POCKETS?

THE OFFER IS A **COURTESY.** WE CAN DISSECT YOU, FIND OUT WHAT MAKES YOU **TICK,** AND CREATE OTHER PEOPLE LIKE YOU.

IF YOU WORK **WITH** US, YOU WON'T WANT FOR **ANYTHING.**

HMMM... ARE WE TALKING **BENEFITS**? HEALTH INSURANCE? MY OWN PARKING SPACE?

I MEAN, I DON'T DRIVE, BUT I LIKE TO BE PREPARED.

AND IF I SAY **NO?**

WE WILL **KILL** NOT ONLY YOU, BUT ALL YOUR FRIENDS, YOUR FAMILY, **ANYONE** YOU EVER CAME IN CONTACT WITH.

WHAT, LIKE **LAST NIGHT?**

HOW'D **THAT** WORK OUT FOR YOU?

105

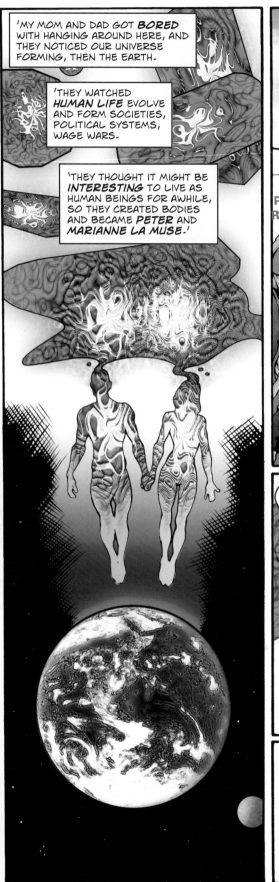

'MY MOM AND DAD GOT **BORED** WITH HANGING AROUND HERE, AND THEY NOTICED OUR UNIVERSE FORMING, THEN THE EARTH.

'THEY WATCHED **HUMAN LIFE** EVOLVE AND FORM SOCIETIES, POLITICAL SYSTEMS, WAGE WARS.

'THEY THOUGHT IT MIGHT BE **INTERESTING** TO LIVE AS HUMAN BEINGS FOR AWHILE, SO THEY CREATED BODIES AND BECAME **PETER** AND **MARIANNE LA MUSE.**'

'THEY LIVED AS AN AMERICAN **HIPPY COUPLE** IN 20TH CENTURY NEW YORK CITY. THEY WORKED AS LAWYERS AND ACTIVISTS, DOING WHAT **HUMANS** DO WHEN THEY'RE TRYING TO HELP THINGS ALONG. THAT WAS THEIR PROJECT. AND THEY GAVE BIRTH TO ME AND MY SISTER LIKE HUMANS DO.

'SO WE'RE BOTH HUMAN **AND** ALIEN. WE KNOW WHAT THEY KNOW.'

END POLICE BRUTALITY

JUSTICE FOR THE HOMELESS!

NO JUSTICE, NO PEACE

JEWISH MYTHOLOGY HAS A NAME FOR IT: 'TORAH IN THE WOMB'.

THE BABY IN THE WOMB IS IN A STATE OF GRACE AND KNOWS EVERYTHING ABOUT THE WORLD, BUT WHEN IT'S BORN, IT **FORGETS**, AND HAS TO LEARN EVERYTHING FROM SCRATCH.

THE DIFFERENCE IS, I **DIDN'T** FORGET AFTER I WAS BORN.

SO YEAH, MY PARENTS MAY BE GONE, BUT **NOW** MY PROJECT IS TO SAVE THE WORLD BEFORE PEOPLE LIKE YOU AND YOUR BOSSES TOTALLY FUCK IT UP!

IT'S FUN, BUT I'M DOING IT ALSO BECAUSE THIS IS MY **HOME** AND WHERE I WAS BORN!

WHAT ABOUT YOUR SISTER...?

LIBBY? TOTALLY **NORMAL.**

IT'S KIND OF A **MYSTERY** WHY AND HOW SHE DIDN'T KEEP HER POWERS.

ONE DAY, WE'LL FIGURE IT OUT.

HM. POOPED HIS **PANTS.**

POOR BABY.

HI, EVERYBODY!

MR. VICE PRESIDENT! HOW'S IT **HANGIN'?**

I'M THE NEW BOSS OF YOU.

IT'S AN ALIEN INVASION... AND WE **CAN'T** STOP HER...

I KNOW **EVERYTHING** ABOUT YOU. BUT YOU ONLY KNOW WHAT I WANT YOU TO KNOW ABOUT ME.

MR. VENKOW CAN TELL YOU ALL ABOUT MY BACKGROUND AND MY PEOPLE.

WE PLAY LONG GAMES.

THIS IS **MINE.**

HEY LIB, READ MY MIND AND DO THE *WITNESS* THING! DID YOU GET EVERYTHING THAT HAPPENED TODAY?

YOU STOPPED TIME INSIDE THAT BUILDING WHILE YOU *TOYED* WITH THE POOR BASTARDS! *VICIOUS*, SUSAN!

AHH, THEY *DESERVED* IT!

YOU *FUCKED* WITH THEM FOR OVER *TEN HOURS* IN THERE, AND OUT HERE IT WAS STILL ONLY *10 AM*...

I HAD TO BE IN *PAKISTAN* TO FUCK UP SOME VILLAGE ELDERS WHO ABUSED A LOCAL GIRL. THEN I HAD A FASHION SHOOT IN *MILAN*.

I DIDN'T WANT TO BE *LATE*.

TELL ME YOU DIDN'T TAKE OVER THE FUCKING *WORLD*!

LATER, I MET WITH THE *UN SECRETARY GENERAL* ABOUT DECLARING MYSELF A COUNTRY.

I READ HIS AURA, AND YOU KNOW, HE'S *SEEN* MY SEX VIDEO!

SUSAN...

THAT'S THE INTERNET FOR YA! YOU NEVER *KNOW* WHO'S GOING TO SEE SOMETHING! IT WAS *HILARIOUS!* HE WAS SUCH A NICE GUY!

SUSAN!

OKAY! WHAT? WHAT *IS* IT?

SOMEONE WANTS A *WORD* WITH YOU!

HOW—? WHY—?

WELL, WE HAD TO GROW OURSELVES **NEW BODIES** SINCE WE LET THE OLD ONES DIE.

WE'D NEVER BEEN HUMAN **CHILDREN** BEFORE, SO WE THOUGHT WE'D GIVE IT A TRY.

THIS IS **OUR** NEW PROJECT!

BUT WHAT ABOUT **YOU**, SUSAN? WHAT HAVE YOU GOT TO SAY FOR YOURSELF?

OKAY— I REALLY CAN EXPLAIN—

SIT!

RIGHT, I'VE ONLY BEEN REACTING TO THE WAY THINGS ARE, **OKAY?**

BY **RIDDING THE WORLD OF OIL?!** THEY'LL **REALLY** WANT TO KILL YOU NOW!

WHAT'LL HAPPEN TO **PLASTICS?** THEY **NEED** OIL TO MAKE PLASTICS! HOW WILL **HOSPITALS** GET NEW EQUIPMENT? WHAT ABOUT **WORKING PEOPLE** WHO NEED THEIR CARS FOR THEIR **LIVELIHOODS?**

CHILL, LIB. I'VE WORKED IT ALL OUT.

I ALREADY INTRODUCED A NATURALLY-OCCURRING **REPLACEMENT** FOR PLASTIC. POLYCARBONS AND POLYMERS THAT AREN'T TOXIC.

WHAT'S THE **POINT** OF PLAYING GOD IF YOU'RE NOT GONNA COVER ALL THE BASES?

SO YOU ARE PLAYING GOD. I **SEE.**

GOD, **NO!** I DON'T **MEAN** IT LIKE THAT!

I DON'T WANT TO RULE THE WORLD! I JUST WANT TO **SAVE** IT!

BY INTIMIDATING THE WORLD'S GOVERNMENTS AND INDUSTRIALISTS?

THEY **DESERVED** TO BE SCARED TO THEIR SENSES!

I **COULD** HAVE TAKEN OVER THE WORLD AND CHANGED EVERYTHING IN ONE AFTERNOON, BUT I DIDN'T, OKAY?

INSTEAD, YOU'RE INITIATING RADICAL CHANGES BY **STEALTH**.

PRETTY MUCH, YEAH.

AFTER AN HOUR OF EXPLANATIONS...

...AND THOSE NEO-NAZIS YOU HAD **SEX** WITH WERE NO BETTER THAN THE ONES YOU **ATOMIZED** —

— WHY DID YOU KILL **THEM** AND SPARE THE REST?

I **SHOULDN'T** HAVE KILLED THEM, BUT I READ THEIR MINDS AND GOT **MAD**, OKAY?

EVEN LATER...

AND HOW DO YOU EXPLAIN **AFRICA**, THEN?

I WANTED THEM TO STOP HAVING TO DEPEND ON MONEY AND CHARITY FROM THE **WEST!** AND THEN THEY CAN STOP BEING **EXPLOITED** AND SORT OUT THEIR OWN PROBLEMS!

AND YOU MADE THEM VIRTUALLY **INVULNERABLE**...

MOM, THEY DESERVE A **BREAK!** THEY'VE BEEN FUCKED OVER SO MUCH THROUGHOUT HISTORY, THIS WAY THEY CAN GET THINGS RIGHT **WITHOUT** MURDERING EACH OTHER!

...WHAT ABOUT THE **CHAOS** YOU'VE PLUNGED THE STOCK MARKETS INTO WITH YOUR DABBLING?

THE MARKETS ARE FIXED AND CORRUPT ANYWAY! THEY **NEED** TO BE KICKED IN THE ASS!

113

I THINK SHE'S THOUGHT IT ALL OUT, PETER. IF SHE *HASN'T*, SHE CAN FIGURE IT OUT.

YES! GOD! THANK YOU!

SUSAN, WE DIDN'T GIVE YOU ENOUGH *CREDIT*. YOU SEEM TO KNOW WHAT YOU'RE DOING...

SO WE'RE GOING TO LET YOU *CONTINUE* ON THIS PROJECT AS YOU SEE FIT.

REALLY? THANKS!

CARRY ON, GIRLS!

WE'RE JUST GOING TO EXPLORE THIS *NEW WORLD* YOU'RE MAKING!

SEE YOU *SOON*!

WHEW!

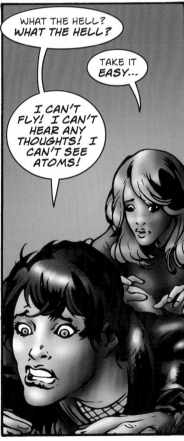

115

I WAS SAYING, "LA MUSE: THE SERIES" WILL BE A **LANDMARK** IN TELEVISION HISTORY!

FEMALE EMPOWERMENT! GIRLS, TEENAGERS AND MOMS LOVE HER! GUYS LOVE HER!

I DUNNO, GUYS... WE **ALREADY** HAVE OFFERS FROM HBO, SHOWTIME, THE BABY CABLERS AND THE OTHER NETS...

YES, BUT WE HAVE THE BIGGEST **RATINGS!**

YOU HAVE OUR WORD THAT WE'LL BE **FAITHFUL** TO SUSAN'S LIFE AND HER MISSION. I ALREADY SUPPORT A **LOT** OF THE CAUSES SHE'S PART OF.

AND SUSAN **HATES** REALITY SHOWS.

OH, WE WANT A SCRIPTED **DRAMA**, NOT A REALITY SHOW!

IT'LL BE OUR **FLAGSHIP** SHOW!

SHE'S GONNA WANT SCRIPT **AND** CAST APPROVAL.

WE CAN **WORK** WITH HER ON THAT.

WE'LL PUT THE BEST SHOWRUNNERS ON IT!

AND WE CAN GET HER ENVIRONMENTAL AND TOLERANCE MESSAGES TO A **WIDER** AUDIENCE!

OKAY, SEND ME THE OFFER IN THE **MORNING**, I'LL RUN IT BY HER.

C'MON, LIBBY, WE'RE OFFERING THE BEST DEAL AND YOU **KNOW** IT!

WE WOULD **LOVE** FOR SUSAN TO JOIN OUR FAMILY.

THE WORLD IS STILL REELING FROM THE SUDDEN **DEPLETION** OF OIL RESERVES AND SUPPLIES A WEEK AGO. JUST AS SUDDENLY, CARS AND VEHICLES WORLDWIDE HAVE BEEN MYSTERIOUSLY **CONVERTED** SO THAT THEY NO LONGER NEED TO RUN ON GASOLINE.

POWER STATIONS AND ELECTRICITY COMPANIES **ALSO** NO LONGER NEED OIL, SUBSISTING ON SOLAR, WIND AND ALTERNATE SOURCES.

SO HERE I AM, PRETENDING THINGS ARE FINE AND DANDY, CARRYING ON AS NORMAL WHILE EVERYTHING'S GOING **BATSHIT.**

STORY OF MY **LIFE**, REALLY.

Chapter 10:
Lost It And Faking It

BOO-HOO-YOU. YOU GOTTA GET UP AND FACE THE **WORLD** SOONER OR LATER.

MY LIFE IS **OVER**... TALK ABOUT PEAKING EARLY...

WHAT AM I GONNA **DO**?! I MADE ALL THOSE COMMITMENTS... TALKS, LECTURES...

KEEP 'EM. NOBODY **KNOWS** YOU LOST YOUR POWERS. I'M NOT GONNA GET DRUNK AND BLAB AGAIN.

IT'S NOT LIKE LYING TO THE PUBLIC IS **NEW** TO YOU.

BUT EVERYTIME I SHOW MY FACE, I'LL FEEL INCOMPLETE, LIKE I'M A TOTAL **FRAUD**!

CONGRATULATIONS. YOU'RE NOW NO DIFFERENT FROM ALL MY **OTHER** CLIENTS.

AND OH MY GOD! I'M GONNA DIE!

WELCOME TO MY WORLD.

HEART ATTACKS! CANCER! I'LL HAVE TO GIVE UP **SMOKING**!

YOU'RE HEALTHY. YOU WON'T DIE FROM NATURAL CAUSES FOR **DECADES**.

YOU HAVE A MUCH BETTER CHANCE OF GETTING **MURDERED** FIRST.

SHIT! THAT'S RIGHT! **BODYGUARDS!** I'LL HAVE TO HIRE BODYGUARDS!

I'LL NEED **MONEY** FOR THAT! I NEVER REALLY NEEDED MONEY BEFORE! I'LL HAVE TO GET A JOB...!

WELL, BEFORE YOU SIGN UP FOR **UNEMPLOYMENT,** TAKE A LOOK AT YOUR LATEST BANK STATEMENT.

OH.

OH! HOLY **SHIT!**

YUP!

ALL YOUR APPEARANCES, SPEAKING ENGAGEMENTS, BOOK DEALS, INTERVIEWS, ENDORSEMENTS, MODELING GIGS...

PEOPLE ARE PAYING YOU A SHITLOAD OF MONEY JUST FOR BEING **YOU.**

BUT I TOLD THEM TO **DONATE** MY FEES TO CHARITIES AND CAUSES!

THAT'S WHY YOU HAVE AN **AGENT.** I NEGOTIATED NOMINAL FEES FOR YOU SEPARATE FROM THE DONATIONS.

EVEN AFTER THE AGENCY'S 10% COMMISSION, MONEY IS THE **LAST** THING YOU NEED TO WORRY ABOUT RIGHT NOW.

ALSO: NOW THAT YOU'RE A SOVEREIGN COUNTRY AND ITS AMBASSADOR, YOU DON'T HAVE TO PAY **TAXES.**

LIBBY! I LOVE YOU!

YEAH, YEAH.

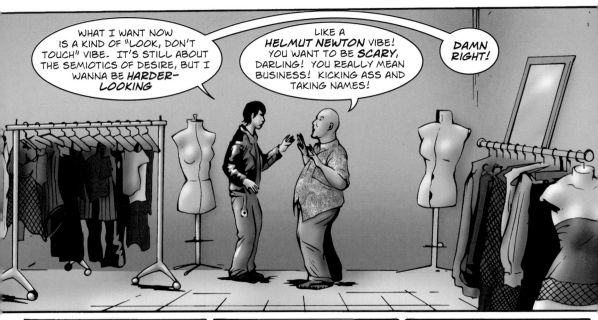

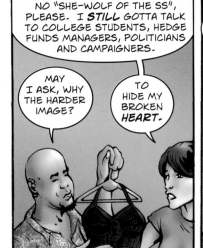

WE'RE LOOKING AT AMERICA *LEAVING* THE WORLD STAGE! IT'S A COMPLETE FREE-FOR-ALL!

NOT EVEN RUSSIA, NOT EVEN *CHINA* LOOK SET TO BECOME THE DOMINANT POWER!

IF YOU'RE CARRYING ANY KEYS, OR GUN, *LEAVE* THEM IN THE TRAY.

HOW IS HE *THIS* WEEK?

SAME OL', SAME OL'. SOMETIMES HE SAYS THAT STUFF ABOUT *MATHEMATICS* AGAIN.

'HER THOUGHTS ARE ALL MATHEMATICS AND POETRY...'

YEAH, I REMEMBER.

SIR?

IT'S ME, *BRADLEY.*

IT'S HAPPENING LIKE YOU **SAID** IT WOULD.

THE STOCK MARKET CRASH, THE **DOLLAR** PLUMMETING, AND NO ONE KNOWS **SHE** CAUSED IT ALL.

NOBODY KNOWS, AND SHE'S HIDING IN **PLAIN SIGHT**, PLAYING A FLUFFY CELEBRITY.

JUST LIKE YOU CALLED IT.

IT'S ALL FALLING APART.

THE MEN AND WOMEN WHO HAVE BEEN KEEPING OUR WORLD **SAFE** FOR COMMERCE AND PROFIT ARE FALLING APART!

THERE'S NO ONE LEFT TO GIVE US ORDERS OR SIGN OUR **PAYCHECKS.**

THE PRESIDENT'S **TERRIFIED.** MOST OF THE COUNCIL ARE DEAD. SOME OF THEM KILLED THEMSELVES.

THE SAUDI MEMBERS ARE ON THE RUN FROM **ASSASSINS**, TRYING TO HOLD ONTO THE MONEY THEY HAVE LEFT.

THERE AREN'T MANY OF US LEFT IN THE TASK FORCE.

BUT WE STILL **BELIEVE** IN YOU, SIR. WE BELIEVE IN THE **MISSION.**

I HAVEN'T RECALLED AGENT **LACKLEY** FROM LA. HE'S STILL UNDERCOVER AS "CASANOVA".

HE'S BEEN PLAYING UP THE FUNDAMENTALISTS WHO THINK SHE'S THE **ANTICHRIST**, GAVE THEM FUNDS AND ARMS TO GO TO LA. MAYBE THEY'LL GET LUCKY.

'SHE'S STILL IN THE PAPERS, THOUGH. MAYBE SHE *IS* HEARTBROKEN. SHE SURE DOESN'T LOOK TOO *HAPPY*.'

'AND WHAT GIVES WITH THE NEW *BODYGUARDS* KEEPING THE ASSHOLES AWAY FROM HER? SHE'S NEVER NEEDED ANYONE TO KEEP 'EM OFF HER BEFORE.'

IT'S TO AVOID LAWSUITS.

'AND SHE HAS AN *ANSWER* FOR EVERYTHING!'

HERE'S ANOTHER THOUGHT: NO ONE HAS SEEN HER *FLYING* FOR OVER A MONTH NOW!

I'M KINDA DEPRESSED. DON'T *FEEL* LIKE FLYING.

A GODDAMMNED ANSWER FOR *EVERYTHING!*

WAAAAAH!

I CAN'T *TAKE* MUCH MORE OF THIS!

I GOTTA GET MY POWERS *BACK!*

UNTIL YOU DO, SUCK IT *UP!*

THE TARGET HAS STEPPED UP HER ACTIVISM IN THE PAST MONTH WHILE HER ACTUAL *FEATS* HAVE COME TO A STOP. WHEN ASKED, SHE SAID IT WAS TIME FOR PEOPLE TO TAKE ACTION *COLLECTIVELY...*

'SHE CONTINUES TO *COMPARTMENTALIZE* HER ACTIVITIES BETWEEN CELEBRITY APPEARANCES AT PREMIERES, AND SERIOUS TALKS AND LECTURES AT COLLEGES AND COMMUNITY CENTERS.'

LET'S GET RID OF *PREDATORY* CAPITALISM, NOT CAPITALISM PER SE! THERE HASN'T BEEN A FREE MARKET FOR *DECADES!* THE CORPORATIONS HAVE BEEN *FIXING* IT!

DECAPITALIZATION IS THE WAY TO GO! REWRITE CAPITALISM SO IT WORKS PROPERLY! WEALTH GETS RE-DISTRIBUTED BY THE *MARKET!*

HER ADVICE TO HEDGE FUNDS IS *ALREADY* REWRITING THE GLOBAL FINANCIAL MAP! WE'RE *FAILING!*

SEE, THAT'S WHAT MOST ACTIVISTS DON'T *GET!* YOU CAN'T GET CORPORATIONS TO STOP WHAT THEY'RE DOING BY MAKING THEM FEEL GUILTY -- *THEY DON'T FEEL GUILTY!*

YOU HIT THEM WHERE IT HURTS: *SHORT THEIR STOCK.* IF THEY START LOSING MONEY DOING BAD THINGS, THEY'LL STOP!

130

IT'S OCCURRED TO ME: *WHY* HAVE PEOPLE BEEN SO ACCEPTING OF LA MUSE'S SUPERHUMAN ABILITIES WITHOUT QUESTIONING THEM OR BEING AFRAID?

COULD SHE HAVE CAST SOME SORT OF *SPELL* OVER EVERYONE'S MINDS? SOME FORM OF MASS HYPNOSIS?

ANYWAY, OUR AGENTS REPORT THAT THERE WILL BE ANOTHER ATTEMPT TO HIT THE TARGET TODAY.

I DON'T EVEN KNOW IF WE SHOULD *BOTHER* ANYMORE... MAYBE WE'LL FINALLY GET LUCKY...

SO YEAH, I'M LIKE HER *BOSWELL*. I FILM HER IN HER ON AND OFF-STAGE, KEEPIN' IT ALL REAL, Y'KNOW?

SO, ER, WHAT ARE YOU DOING LATER?

WHAT STILL BUMS ME OUT IS THAT MORE PEOPLE ARE INTO THE CELEBRITY GOSSIP SHIT THAN THE *ACTIVISM*...

WELL, THE CDS AND DVDS OF YOUR LECTURES AND TALKS ARE *STILL* SELLING, SO YOU'RE GETTING THE MESSAGE OUT.

SIGH! I *KNOW*, BUT...

WHAT YOU NEED IS ANOTHER INCIDENT WHERE YOU SAVE EVERYONE'S ASS!

GOD, TODD! I DON'T NEED ANOTHER NUTCASE WITH A BOMB, NOT *NOW*—

SUSAN LA MUSE!

131

EEEEEEE!

EVERYONE STAY CALM!

MS. LA MUSE! KEEP BACK!

M—MINE EYES HAVE SEEN THE GLORY... YEA, THOUGH I WALK THROUGH THE VALLEY OF **DEATH**...

HEY!

THE LORD IS MY SHEPHARD, I SHALL NOT...

HEY!

BONK!

OWW!

AAA!

I'VE LEFT YOU GUYS ALONE BECAUSE IT'S **FREE SPEECH**, Y'KNOW? YOU CAN CALL ME ANYTHING YOU WANT, STICKS AND STONES.

BUT WHEN YOU START GETTING IN MY **FACE**, WE'RE GONNA HAVE **WORDS**.

YOU WANNA BELIEVE A BOOK THAT WAS WRITTEN BY **BABYLONIAN CULTISTS** AND TRANSLATED BY A BUNCH OF ENGLISH POETS IS **DIVINE TRUTH**, BE MY GUEST!

BUT WHERE'S IT SAY YOU GOTTA KILL ANYONE YOU DON'T LIKE? HAVE YOU ACTUALLY **READ** THE BIBLE?

YOU'VE SEEN THE NEWS. YOU **KNOW** WHAT I CAN DO.

YOU'RE NOT GONNA KILL ME OR **ANYONE** TODAY.

YOU'RE JUST GONNA KILL **YOURSELF**, AND IT'LL JUST MEAN YOU'RE AN **IDIOT**.

133

BUT YOU KNOW WHAT I'M GONNA DO? I'M GONNA BRING YOU BACK TO LIFE, GOOD AS NEW, SO THAT EVERYONE CAN SEE WHAT A FREAKIN' MORON YOU ARE AND *LAUGH* AT YOU.

ON NATIONAL TELEVISION.

SEE THESE GUYS? THEY'RE *EX-COMMANDOS* FROM ISRAEL. I DIDN'T HIRE THEM JUST FOR ME, THEY'RE FOR EVERYONE AROUND ME.

NOW PUT THAT SHIT DOWN BEFORE I HAVE THEM STUFF IT UP YOUR SORRY ASS AND KREV MAGA YOU INTO A PRETZEL!

HOT *DAMN,* SUSAN! WE HAVE OUR NEXT VIDEO CLIP!

PFFT! PIECE OF CAKE!

OH MY FUCKING GOD!

I ACTUALLY *FAKED* HIM OUT!

I THOUGHT I WAS *SOOOOO FUCKING DEAD!*

SO WHO SAYS YOU'RE NOT AN *ACTRESS?*

Chapter 11:
Waiting For Everything To Go Wrong...

MEANWHILE, THE *HATERS* WERE STILL OUT IN FORCE. IT WAS LIKE THEY INSTINCTIVELY *KNEW* THAT SUSAN WAS RESPONSIBLE FOR THE WORLD BEING PLUNGED INTO CHAOS.

SUSAN SAID THEY WERE SPURRED ON BY THE CONSPIRACY THAT WAS OUT TO GET HER.

ANTI-CHRIST

CORRUPTER OF YOUTH

IT'S A GOOD THING THEY DON'T KNOW SHE'S CURRENTLY *POWERLESS.*

SHE IS A GODLESS *LESBIAN* WHO'S TURNING OUR CHILDREN INTO HOMOSEXUALS AND *SLUTS!*

WE SHOULD TURN HER LEFTIST WEAPONS *AGAINST* HER!

BOYCOTT HER! PROTEST LONG AND LOUD AGAINST HER!

I'M OPENING ANOTHER BOTTLE...

WHY DO YOU STILL WATCH THIS ANYWAY?

'KNOW THINE ENEMY', LIB.

HERE'S THE THING:

IT'S ASSHOLES WHO HATE YOU, SO THE KIDS ALL THINK YOU'RE *COOL!* IT'S ALL OXYGEN OF PUBLICITY, BABY!

UNTIL ONE OF 'EM TRIES TO *KILL* YOU AGAIN!

I'M NOT WORRIED!

AS LONG AS SUSAN IS NEAR-OMNIPOTENT, I KNOW I'M *SAFE!*

I INTERVIEWED HER THIS WEEK. SOMETHING'S **UP**. I THINK SHE'S SLIPPING... SHOWING VULNERABILITY...

PART OF MY JOB IS TO READ THE **ENTRAILS** OF CELEBRITY GOSSIP, AND SOMETHING'S NOT NORMAL!

SHE HASN'T BEEN SEEN FLYING FOR **MONTHS** NOW, AND SHE'S NEVER WITHOUT BODYGUARDS WHEN SHE'S OUT IN PUBLIC.

I KNOW WHAT YOU MEAN. LOOK, ANYTHING YOU FIND OUT, WE'D **LOVE** TO HEAR IT!

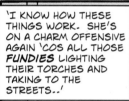

'I KNOW HOW THESE THINGS WORK. SHE'S ON A CHARM OFFENSIVE AGAIN 'COS ALL THOSE **FUNDIES** LIGHTING THEIR TORCHES AND TAKING TO THE STREETS..'

'SHE SPILLED SOME PRE-SCREENED PERSONAL THING SO READERS WOULD FEEL SORRY FOR HER. IT WAS THE USUAL **PRE-FAB CRAP** APPROVED BY A PUBLICIST.'

WELL, I ALWAYS **PLANNED** TO STEP BACK AFTER THE FIRST YEAR AND JUST LET THINGS PLAY OUT. I'M NOT OUT TO BE BOSS OF THE WORLD.

YEAH, YEAH, ENOUGH OF THAT CAMPAIGNING SHIT. WHAT ABOUT YOUR **PERSONAL LIFE?** IS IT TRUE YOU AND CHAD SPLIT UP?

YEAH... BRAD AND I BROKE UP BECAUSE I WAS TOO BUSY WITH THE CAMPAIGNING, AND HE WAS BUSY WITH HIS **MOVIES**... WE JUST DRIFTED APART...

I HAVEN'T SEEN HIM SINCE I WENT TO THE **WOODY ALLEN** REMAKE OF "ZOMBIE HOLOCAUST".

'I CAN'T QUITE PUT MY FINGER ON IT, BUT WHY DO I GET THE FEELING THAT SHE ALSO SUBTLY CHANGED THE WORLD IN **SMALL WAYS** ON TOP OF THE BIG STUFF...?'

THAT MISSILE'S GONNA HIT THE ISLAND IN FOUR MINUTES UNLESS I GET TO IT!

THIS IS GONNA TOTALLY SUCK!

GOD, I MISS FLYING!

MAAAN--- THAT HAYLEY McGRATH IS *HOT!*

WHAT DID YOU *THINK* WHEN THEY CAST HER TO PLAY YOU, SUSAN?

'THOSE BREASTS *CAN'T* BE REAL!'

BE NICE!

OKAY! BREAK FOR LUNCH!

HOW DO YOU LIKE IT *SO* FAR, SUSAN? ISN'T HAYLEY *AMAZING?*

SHE'S COOL! I DON'T KNOW MUCH ABOUT TV, BUT YOU GUYS ARE DOIN' *GREAT!*

YOU WOULDN'T *BELIEVE* THE BUZZ THE SHOW IS ALREADY GETTING! WE'VE PRE-SOLD IT TO VIRTUALLY *EVERY* MARKET WORLDWIDE!

139

THE NETWORK SAYS THEY'RE GONNA MAKE "LA MUSE" THEIR *FLAGSHIP SHOW* NEXT SEASON!

IT'S ALL A CRAPSHOOT. THEY MIGHT *HATE* THE PILOT AND IT NEVER AIRS.

THAT'S *USUALLY* WHAT HAPPENS.

HAYLEY? YOU'RE NEEDED BACK ON THE SET!

---AND *THAT* IS THE SECRET TO FLYING.

YEAH... I *GET* IT NOW!

I GOTTA GET MY HAIR AND MAKE-UP RETOUCHED!

I'LL CALL YOU!

ABOUT DAMN TIME! I HAVE TO GET BACK TO THE OFFICE! YOU'RE NOT MY *ONLY* CLIENT, YOU KNOW!

YOU *MADE OUT* WITH THE ACTRESS WHO'S PLAYING YOU! HOW MESSED UP IS *THAT!*

THESE DAYS, I GET MY JOLLIES WHERE I *CAN*, LIB.

YOU'RE SUCH A NARCISSIST!

BANG! BANG!

BANG!

GET HIM! GET HIM!

GET HIS GUN! SHIT!

SUSAN! ARE YOU–?

ARRRRGGGH!

BULLETPROOF HELD UP. I THINK THE CERAMIC PLATE'S CRACKED...

OH THANK GOD! DOES IT HURT?

LIKE A MOTHER-FUCKER!

...POLICE BELIEVE HE SNUCK ONTO THE LOT THROUGH THE STUDIO TOUR AND MADE HIS WAY TO LA MUSE!

I LOVE HER! SOB! IF I CAN'T HAVE HER, NO ONE CAN!

HE WASN'T JUST A STALKER! THEY PUT HIM IN MY WAY!

OW!

WE HAVE TO GET YOU BETTER BODYGUARDS! THOSE TWO TOTALLY DROPPED THE BALL!

GUYS!

WHY DIDN'T YOU CALL ME?

OH, HEY, TIM. WHAT'S DONE IS DONE...

OKAY, LET'S THINK ABOUT THIS...

PEOPLE WOULD'VE BEEN SUSPICIOUS IF THEY DIDN'T GET TO SEE THE SHOOTING.

THAT FUCKING TODD LEAKED THE TAPE!

IT'S ALL SHOW BUSINESS...

SIR, I'D LIKE YOU TO HAVE A LOOK AT THIS...

THE ISRAELI-PALESTINIAN ALLIANCE HAS OFFERED TO *MEDIATE* IN THE CONFLICT IN SAUDI ARABIA. THE SAUDI ROYAL FAMILY ARE STILL IN HIDING, BUT...

THIS IS LAST NIGHT'S NEWS... I'LL JUST FAST-FORWARD IT...

A STALKER TRIED TO KILL HER, AND HE *FAILED*, OF COURSE.

PLEASE, SIR... IS THIS GETTING *THROUGH* TO YOU?

HER HEDGE FUNDS ARE BUYING UP GOLD, SILVER, COPPER, PRECIOUS METALS. THERE'S ALREADY A SHIFT *AWAY* FROM PETROLEUM-BASED PRODUCTS WORLDWIDE, AND ALL THE NEW ALTERNATE PRODUCTS AND MATERIALS HAVE BEEN PATENTED IN LA MUSE'S NAME.

NGGGGGHHH!

FOR GOD'S SAKE! IT'S STARING US ALL IN THE FACE!

WHY AM I THE ONLY ONE WHO *SEES* THIS?

BAM! BAM!

SIR! STOP IT!

SIR?!

NO BULLET'S *EVER* MADE CONTACT WITH HER BODY BEFORE! SHE COULD *WILL* THEM AWAY! SHE USED HER *MIND* TO PROTECT HERSELF! SHE DIDN'T SEE THIS COMING!

BUT THAT BULLET HIT HER!

SHE'S-LOST-HER-POWERS!

SIGN ME OUT OF HERE!

GET THIS THING OFF ME!

GET ME CLEAN CLOTHES AND FRESH DIAPERS!

WE HAVE WORK TO DO!

IT'S GOOD TO HAVE YOU *BACK*, SIR!

WE FINALLY HAVE A CHANCE TO WIPE HER OUT ONCE AND FOR ALL! WE HAVE TO TAKE IT *NOW*!

SIR, IF THIS IS *TRUE*...

OF COURSE IT'S TRUE! THAT ATTACK TOOK HER BY *SURPRISE*! DIDN'T YOU SEE THAT LOOK ON HER FACE?

PUT THE *WORD* OUT! CONTACT THE MEDIA! I WANT TV COVERAGE! OP-EDS! FEATURE ARTICLES! AND TELL OUR ALLIES!

YES, SIR!

POWERLESS?

Did Ann Coulter have Bill O'Reilley's love-child?

'LET'S LOOK AT THE FACTS: NO ONE HAS SEEN HER FLYING FOR THE LAST THREE MONTHS. SHE HAS HIRED BODYGUARDS TO FOLLOW HER AROUND. SHE'S MOSTLY BEEN TALKING.'

'COULD IT BE THAT SHE DOESN'T HAVE HER POWERS ANYMORE? THAT SHE'S A NORMAL LIKE THE REST OF US? IF SHE IS, THEN SHE'S NOTHING SPECIAL. SHE'S JUST ANOTHER SPOILED CELEBRITY DRUNK ON FAME.'

ALLLLRIGHT! THIS IS WHAT I WAS *BORN* TO DO!

THAT PINNEY BITCH!

YOU COULD SAY THIS WAS THE BEGINNING OF THE *END*...

LIBBY, IS IT *TRUE* ABOUT SUSAN'S POWERS?

SHE DOESN'T TELL ME *EVERYTHING*, DICK. SHE'S A LAW UNTO HERSELF.

THE THING IS, THIS DOESN'T DILUTE HER BRAND NAME AT ALL. IN FACT, SHE'S GETTING EVEN *MORE* POPULAR FROM THE PUBLIC SYMPATHY!

AND ALL THE GREEN CAMPAIGNS AND VENTURES SHE'S INVOLVED IN ARE REALLY *BOOMING* NOW.

OH, YES.

THEY'LL KEEP BOOMING EVEN *WITHOUT* HER NOW.

OF COURSE DICK'S HAPPY. HE AND HIS WIFE ARE MAJOR *INVESTORS* IN THOSE VENTURES. THE DICKS OF THIS WORLD ARE ALWAYS GOING TO SURVIVE.

SO IT'S *TRUE*, THEN? THAT EXPLAINS WHY YOU HAVEN'T COME OVER TO VISIT. I THOUGHT YOU WERE JUST *BUSY*.

I *WAS* BUSY. AND POWERLESS. COULDN'T FLY.

IS IT *PERMANENT*?

I DON'T KNOW YET. LISTEN, IF THE TABLOIDS CALL, TELL 'EM WHATEVER YOU WANT. YOU COULD BUY YOUR *MOM* SOMETHING WITH THE MONEY

SOD THAT! ANYWAY, WHATEVER WHAMMY YOU PUT OUT IS STILL *WORKIN'*. I HAVEN'T SEEN ANY PAPARAZZI OR KILLERS ABOUT.

THAT'S A RELIEF.

146

SIR, SHE'S ON THE MOVE!

HAVE EYES ON THE STREET! TRACK THEIR CELL PHONES! CREDIT CARD, ATM TRANSACTIONS!

ALREADY ON IT, SIR!

THERE WAS A LARGE *ATM* WITHDRAWAL OFF SUNSET. ONE SPOTTER SAID THEY CHECKED INTO A MOTEL SOMEWHERE IN HOLLYWOOD, THEN WE LOST THEM THIS MORNING AS THEY WERE HEADED INTO *GANG* TERRITORY.

DAMMIT! WE DON'T HAVE ANY PEOPLE IN THERE!

OH *COOL!* YOU HAVE ORGANIC FRUITS! AND NUTS!

WHAT YOU SEE'S WHAT YOU GET.

...YEAH, LET STEVE BESHEVSKY HANDLE THE LUCASFILM DEAL. HE WAS *PISSED* AT ME FOR SNATCHING IT FROM UNDER HIM ANYWAY.

OH, AND LIBBY, I'VE GOT KELLY MCGREGOR HOLDING FOR YOU.

PUT HER ON.

LIBBY! IS IT *TRUE?* ARE YOU DRIVING SUSAN AWAY TO A SECLUDED SPOT FOR HER *LAST STAND?*

BOY, WORD SURE TRAVELS *FAST!*

SO *IS* IT TRUE? SHE *LOST* HER POWERS?

SORRY IF THIS MESSES UP THE *SERIES.*

AND YOU *HAVE?* A MISSED PAYMENT FOR YOUR GYM MEMBERSHIP *ISN'T* SUFFERING! GETTING DUMPED BY CRAPPY BOYFRIENDS *ISN'T* SUFFERING! GETTING PASSED OVER FOR PROMOTION *ISN'T* SUFFERING!

I NEVER CLAIMED I *WAS* SUFFERING! I KNOW THE DIFFERENCE! AS AN AMERICAN MIDDLE-CLASS WOMAN, IT'S PART OF MY *CHARACTER* TO BITCH AND MOAN!

SO YOU PICKED A JOB WHERE YOU HAVE TO BE AN *ASSHOLE* BECAUSE YOU'RE DEALING WITH ASSHOLES ALL THE TIME! THAT'S *FUCKED!*

IT MADE IT POSSIBLE FOR ME TO AFFORD THE NICE CAR I'M DRIVING YOU TO YOUR FUCKING *DESTINY* IN!

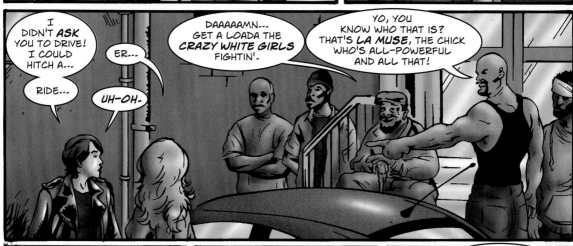

I DIDN'T *ASK* YOU TO DRIVE! I COULD HITCH A...

RIDE...

ER...

UH-OH.

DAAAAAMN... GET A LOADA THE *CRAZY WHITE GIRLS* FIGHTIN'.

YO, YOU KNOW WHO THAT IS? THAT'S *LA MUSE*, THE CHICK WHO'S ALL-POWERFUL AND ALL THAT!

SO YOU THINK YOU *ALL THAT*, GIRL? WALTZIN' INTO OUR NEIGHBORHOOD AND TEARIN' UP THE PEACE WITH YOUR *BITCHING?*

MOTHERFUCKER, I'LL BITCH *ANYWHERE* I WANT! *WHENEVER* I WANT! AT *WHOEVER* I WANT!

SUSAN... DON'T PROVOKE HIM...

HAAAAHAAAAA! C'MERE, YOU CRAZY *BITCH!*

DUUUUUUDE! BEAR HUG!

HOW'S YOUR MOM?

SHE *GOOD!* YOU BETTER STAY PUT, 'COS SHE BAKING *YOU* A *PIE!*

WHOLE NEIGHBOR-HOOD'S COMIN' OUT TO SEE YOU!

WAIT -- SO YOU **KNOW** THIS GUY?

LIB, THIS IS **MARLON DOOLEY.** HE'S AN EX-BLOOD, NOW HE'S THE LOCAL YOUTH WORKER AND LIAISON!

ANY MOTHER-FUCKERS COME LOOKIN' FOR YOU, ME AND MY CREW, WE GOT YOUR **BACK!**

HUH.

IT WAS LIKE **EVERYBODY** SHOWED UP FOR THE BLOCK PARTY. PEOPLE CAME OUT AND HUGGED HER AND GAVE HER FOOD.

THERE WAS ALWAYS A **MOTHER** WHOSE HEALTH SHE RESTORED, A **COMMUNITY CENTER** SHE BUILT, A **SON** SHE TALKED OUT OF CRIME, A **FATHER** SHE REUNITED WITH FAMILY.

SHE KNEW HER ENEMIES WOULDN'T DARE COME INTO THESE NEIGHBORHOODS, THE **RACISTS.**

BUT SHE ALSO KNEW SHE **COULDN'T** HIDE AMONG ORDINARY PEOPLE. SHE WAS HERE TO HAVE ONE LAST PARTY.

SHE WAS HERE TO SAY GOODBYE.

151

IT WAS LIKE SHE WASN'T PLANNING ON COMING OUT OF THIS *ALIVE.* SHE WAS HEADING IN THE FINAL ACT OF A MOVIE. KELLY WOULD *LOVE* TO HEAR ABOUT THIS SCENE.

TOO BAD WE WON'T BE AROUND TO *TELL* HER ABOUT IT.

YOU COULD'VE *SAID* YOU ALREADY KNEW EVERYONE...

WHAT, AND RUIN THE *SUSPENSE?*

YOU KNOW THINGS AREN'T GONNA BE THIS *ROSY* ONCE WE'RE OUT IN THE BOONIES, RIGHT?

DON'T BE SO *NEGATIVE,* LIB!

I'M NOT BEING NEGATIVE! THE WHOLE REASON WE'RE ON THE RUN IS BECAUSE PEOPLE *HATE* YOU!

WELL, D'UH!

SO WHAT ARE YOU GONNA *DO* WHEN WE GET OUT TO THE MIDDLE OF NOWHERE?

I DUNNO... STAY ALIVE LONG ENOUGH FOR ME TO FIGURE OUT HOW TO GET MY POWERS BACK?

ON, THAT'S A *GREAT* PLAN! WE'RE SUPPOSED TO BE GOOD AT THINKING THINGS THROUGH.

POOR SUSAN...

AND PEOPLE ACTUALLY *LOVE* HER!

WELL, SHE REALLY *HAS* BEEN MAKING A DIFFERENCE IN PEOPLE'S LIVES, JUST LIKE WE *TAUGHT* HER.

HER PLAN IS VERY *INTERESTING*, THOUGH, TO RADICALLY OVERHAUL THE ENTIRE ECONOMY AND BANKING SYSTEM.

BUT SHE *DISOBEYED* US. SHE'S SLOWLY ALTERING THE HUMANS WITHOUT THEM KNOWING IT.

EVENTUALLY, THEY COULD EVOLVE TO BECOME LIKE *US*.

I'M ALMOST TEMPTED TO *LET* HER, JUST TO SEE HOW THINGS TURN OUT ...

NOW NOW, WE MADE THIS DECISION *TOGETHER*. NO BACKING OUT NOW.

TOO BAD SHE HAS TO *DIE*!

OH, WELL.

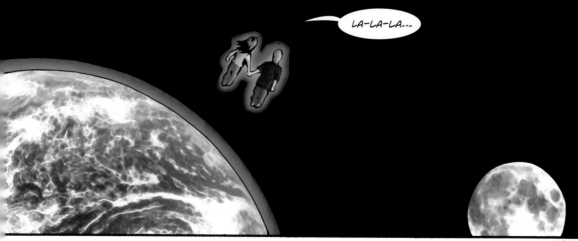

LA-LA-LA...

Chapter 12: The Doomed Celebrity's Road to Nowhere

HI! CAN WE GET A ROOM?

WE'LL PAY *CASH!*

HOPE YOU HAVE FRESH SHEETS AND TOWELS.

Y-YES! YES I DO! ROOM *42!* BEST SUITE WE GOT!

WHY, THANK YOU, CHARLIE! YOU'RE SO *SWEET!*

1987

ANYTHING I CAN *DO* FOR YOU LADIES, JUST CALL THE FRONT DESK AND ASK FOR CHARLIE!

I HOPE HE'S NOT GOING TO SNEAK IN AND RAPE AND DISMEMBER US...

YOU ARE SUCH A NASTY *CITY BITCH* WITH YOUR 'HILLS HAVE EYES' STEREOTYPES!

MOTEL

AHHHHH!

CHARLIE MAY LOOK A LITTLE WEATHER-WORN, BUT HE'S A KIND AND *GENTLE* SOUL WHO MEANS US NO HARM!

HOW DO YOU KNOW *THAT?*

HE'S WATCHED MY SEX TAPE! I COULD *TELL!*

EVERYONE WHO SAW IT HAD THEIR *BRAINS* ALTERED. THEY'RE NOW ENLIGHTENED AND NICE!

155

SO HOW MANY PEOPLE HAVE **SEEN** THAT TAPE?

WELL, JUDGING FROM THE ONES WHO WATCHED THE DVD AND THE ONES WHO DOWNLOADED IT OFF THE 'NET...

WE'RE TALKING A COUPLE **TENS OF MILLIONS** WORLDWIDE.

GOOD GOD!

AND YET, PEOPLE **STILL** WANT TO KILL YOU.

THEY'RE THE ONES WHO **HAVEN'T** SEEN IT.

HUH.

JUST THINK: IF **EVERY** ADULT SAW THAT TAPE, THE WORLD WOULD BE AT PEACE RIGHT NOW AND **NO ONE** WOULD BE TRYING TO KILL ME!

THAT'D BE JUST GREAT.

BUT IT **AIN'T** THE CASE AND WE'RE ON THE RUN. WHAT NOW?

I THOUGHT I'D TRY TO GET MY **POWERS** BACK AND PUT EVERYTHING BACK TOGETHER AGAIN.

AND MOM AND DAD WILL PROBABLY COME AFTER YOU AGAIN. WHAT **THEN?**

I'LL... **TALK** TO THEM?

WHAT MAKES YOU THINK THEY WON'T **KILL** YOU?

C'MON! THEY WOULDN'T DO *THAT!*

THEY TOOK AWAY YOUR POWERS JUST TO FUCK WITH YOU! THEY'RE NOT *HUMAN* ANYMORE!

THEY WEREN'T HUMAN FOR *BILLIONS* OF YEARS BEFORE THEY CAME TO EARTH TO BE HUMAN!

THEY WENT BACK TO WHAT THEY WERE BEFORE, AND WE HAVE *NO IDEA* HOW FUCKING SCARY THAT IS!

NOT TO MENTION THERE'S SHIT GOING DOWN THAT WE *DON'T KNOW* ABOUT! WHAT WAS UP WITH THOSE TWO INSTANCES OF OUR PEOPLE TRYING TO COME THROUGH TO THIS UNIVERSE?

I'VE BEEN WONDERING ABOUT THAT MYSELF!

THEY COULDN'T COME THROUGH AND THEY *DIED.*

UGGGHHHH...!

YOU'RE UP EARLY!

AARRRGH! IT'S NOT WORKING!

YOU'RE SUPPOSED TO BE **CONCENTRATING**, NOT TAKING A DUMP.

HEIGHTENED STATE! WHAT KIND OF HEIGHTENED STATE? FEAR? ANXIETY? SEXUAL AROUSAL? SHIT!

DON'T TELL ME YOU'RE GOING TO BONK CHARLIE THE DESK CLERK.

NO. I DIDN'T BRING ANY **CONDOMS**, AND I CAN'T RISK CATCHING ANY DISEASES.

MAN, WITHOUT POWERS, YOU'RE A FLAMING **HYPO-CHONDRIAC!**

FUCK IT! I'M GOING TO MASTURBATE!

TOO MUCH INFORMATION, SUSAN!

SIR! TARGET *LEFT* LOS ANGELES CITY LIMITS LATE LAST NIGHT! LAST TRAFFIC CAMERAS CAUGHT HER SISTER'S CAR HEADING OUT ON THE 101 FREEWAY!

SO SWITCH TO THE SATELLITES AND DON'T *BOTHER* ME UNTIL THEY TURN UP!

AND GET THE *PSY-OP* IN PLACE! RAAAAARRGH!

YEAH, I'M PRETTY *AT PEACE* WITH BEING LA MUSE'S VIDEOGRAPHER. IT'S GIVEN ME A CAREER, AND THE PAY'S PRETTY GOOD.

I'M AT HER BECK-AND-CALL, BUT SHE'S A FIRM BUT *FAIR* BOSS.

DO YOU KNOW WHERE SHE'S *GONE?*

NAH. I'M AT HER BECK-AND-CALL, BUT IT'S BEEN MORE THAN A *DAY* SINCE I HEARD FROM HER...

MY MAN, WHAT IF I WERE TO TELL YOU THAT WE'RE ABOUT TO ENTER LA MUSE'S *LAST ACT?*

YYYYEAH...?

YOU KNOW HOW THE BRIGHTEST STARS *FLAME OUT* IN THE END. WOULDN'T YOU LIKE TO BE THERE TO CATCH IT ALL ON CAMERA? AFTER ALL, YOU WERE THE ONE RIGHT AT THE BEGINNING.

I'M IN!

159

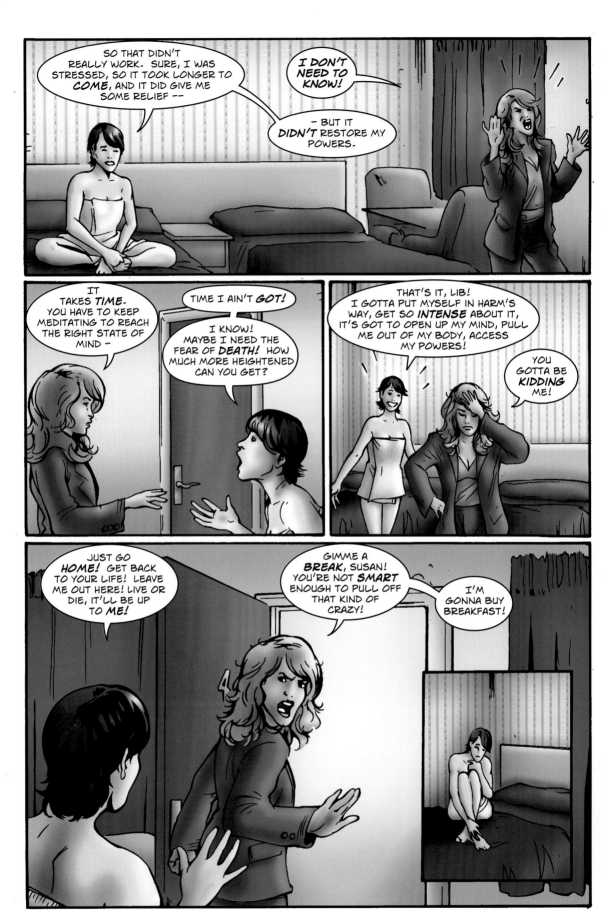

160

SUSAN IS JUST AT A RETREAT RECHARGING HER BATTERIES. SHE'S *EXHAUSTED* HERSELF FROM MORE THAN A YEAR'S CAMPAIGNING AND TRAVELING...

SHE'S VERY TOUCHED BY ALL THE CARDS AND WELL-WISHES...

BULL-FUCKING-SHIT!

SHE'S EITHER HAVING A *NERVOUS BREAKDOWN* OR IN REHAB!

IF I COULD FIND OUT WHERE SHE IS, I COULD WRITE THE *EXPOSÉ* THAT *ENDS* HER RIGHT NOW!

ER, YOUR PHONE...

HEYYY, NAOMI! AM I CALLING YOU TOO LATE?

SUSAN?!

NO! NO! NOT AT *ALL!* EVERYONE'S BEEN WONDERING WHERE YOU DISAPPEARED TO!

IT'S *HER?*

WE'RE ALL KINDA *WORRIED,* AFTER EVERYTHING YOU'VE DONE!

YEAH, I REALIZED THAT.

I WONDERED IF YOU'D LIKE TO DO AN *EXCLUSIVE PHONE* INTERVIEW, Y'KNOW, TO SET EVERYONE AT EASE.

SHIT, *YEAH!* THAT'D BE AMAZING! WHEN DO YOU WANNA DO IT?

I FIGURE TOMORROW MORNING, WHEN WE'RE ALL FRESH AND BRIGHT, Y'KNOW?

I KNOW IT'S *LATE,* YOU GOT YOUR OWN LIFE, AND I'VE BEEN HAVING AN EMOTIONAL TIME...

I JUST WANNA TELL EVERYONE ABOUT WHERE I'M AT... I'VE BEEN MEDITATING AND THINKING A LOT... TAKING STOCK OF MY LIFE... I'M GONNA ENTER A *NEW PHASE* WHEN I GET BACK!

YEAH... YEAH... YEAH...

I'LL WRITE IT ALL IN MY MOST *DEATHLESS* PROSE!

ATTAGIRL! THANKS, NAY!

NO, THANK *YOU*, SUSAN!

HA! I'VE SEEN THIS *HUNDREDS* OF TIMES BEFORE!

BRIGHT YOUNG THING BECOMES FLAVOR-OF-THE-MONTH AND EVERYONE *LOVES* HER. SHE'S ON TV, MAGAZINE COVERS, EVERYONE WANTS A PIECE OF HER. SHE GETS *ADDICTED* TO FAME, SCREWS UP *BIG!*

THIS IS IT! HER FLAME-OUT! HER SELL-BY DATE! I FINALLY GET MY *REVENGE!* ISN'T IT *GREAT?*

OH, YEAH!

NOW THE GUY SHE'S WITH CAN START TRACKING ME, AND THEY'LL BE ONTO ME BY *TOMORROW.*

I STILL CAN'T BELIEVE YOU'RE GOING *THROUGH* WITH THIS...

165

WELL, **THIS** LOOKS DESERTED ENOUGH! NO INNOCENT BYSTANDERS OUT HERE!

I CAN'T **BELIEVE** YOU'RE GOING THROUGH WITH THIS!

THERE'S **NO** GUARANTEE YOUR POWERS WILL COME BACK!

I CAN'T THINK OF ANYTHING **ELSE** TO DO.

THANKS FOR DRIVING ME ALL THE WAY, LIB. YOU CAN GO BACK TO **LA** AND GET ON WITH YOUR LIFE NOW.

NO WAY! I'M STICKING WITH YOU TILL THE **END**!

WHAT **FOR**? THERE'S NOTHING HERE FOR YOU!

I'M THE **WITNESS**, REMEMBER?

AND YOU'RE MY **SISTER**! WHO ELSE HAVE YOU GOT?

BUT THERE'S NO **POINT** YOU STAYING OUT HERE!

YOU **SAID** THIS WAS GONNA BE ALL OR NOTHING!

WELL, IT'LL BE ALL OR NOTHING FOR **ME** TOO!

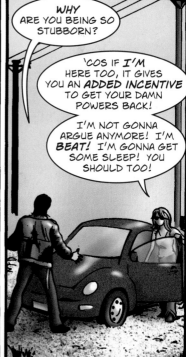

WHY ARE YOU BEING SO STUBBORN?

'COS IF **I'M** HERE TOO, IT GIVES YOU AN **ADDED INCENTIVE** TO GET YOUR DAMN POWERS BACK!

I'M NOT GONNA ARGUE ANYMORE! I'M **BEAT**! I'M GONNA GET SOME SLEEP! YOU SHOULD TOO!

THAT'S **HER!**

HELLO, NAOMI'S PHONE.

WHERE'S NAOMI?

SHE'S INDISPOSED RIGHT NOW. CAN I TAKE A MESSAGE?

I **KNOW** WHO YOU ARE, LACKLEY. AND NAOMI WOULD RATHER **DIE** THAN LET ANYONE HOLD HER PHONE FOR HER.

THAT ONLY MEANS **ONE THING.**

SO WHAT ARE YOU SO **UPSET** ABOUT?

SHE ABSOLUTELY HATED YOUR GUTS AND WANTED TO **DESTROY** YOU.

LISTEN, ASSHOLE, SHE MAY HAVE BEEN PETTY, VINDICTIVE, SELFISH, HAD BAD JUDGMENT AND ALWAYS MISSED THE BIG PICTURE...

...BUT SHE WAS STILL MY **FRIEND.**

YOU SEE ME AGAIN, THAT'S **WHY.**

REMEMBER THAT.

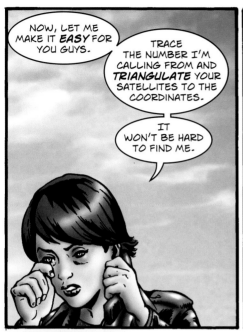

ALL OR
NOTHING...

171

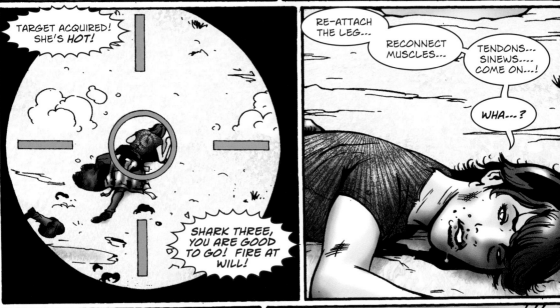

INITIATE ELECTRO-STIMULATION TO RESTART HEART...

FIRE UP SYNAPSES TO RESTORE MEMORY AND BRAIN ACTIVITY...

AAAAAAAKKKKK!

RELEASE ENDORPHINS TO DAMPEN PAIN AND MENTAL TRAUMA...

INDUCE SLEEP TO COMPLETE HEALING CYCLE.

AAAAAHHHH...

I'LL BE RIGHT BACK, LIB.

HMMM... YOU'RE **PRIVATE CONTRACTORS.**

OH MY GOD... OH MY GOD...

THAT MEANS I WOULDN'T FEEL AS BAD IF I DO **HORRIBLE THINGS** TO YOU.

WE CAN'T TAKE HER! GET US OUT OF HERE!

NOW! NOW! NOW!

DON'T - KKKK! - DON'T KILL ME...

THE PUBLIC REALLY OUGHTTA **KNOW** THIS...

STOP FILMING ME, TODD.

OKAY.

THANKEW! NOW LET'S SEE WHAT YOU'VE BEEN SHOOTING.

184

LOOK, I'M THE ONE WHO MADE YOU FAMOUS IN THE FIRST PLACE! I'M LIKE YOUR *CONSCIENCE*, RIGHT? I KEEP YOU HUMAN! YOU'RE *STILL* HUMAN, RIGHT? PLEASE DON'T KILL ME...

TODD...

YOUR CAMERAWORK SUCKS, YOU HAVE NO SENSE OF FRAMING, YOUR EDITING HAS NO RHYTHM, AND YOU HAVE THE ETHICS OF A *VENEREAL DISEASE*.

YOU'RE *FIRED*.

YOU CAN HITCH A RIDE HOME FIVE MILES SOUTH OF HERE.

OKAY...

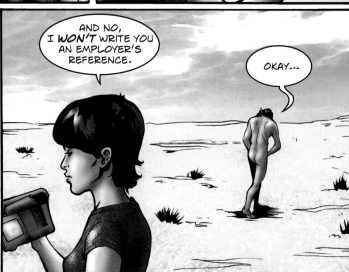

AND NO, I *WON'T* WRITE YOU AN EMPLOYER'S REFERENCE.

OKAY...

SUSAN!

HEY, LIB. FEELING *BETTER?*

WE HAVE TO TALK! IT'S *IMPORTANT!*

HOLD ON, LIB! I STILL HAVE SOME *LOOSE ENDS* TO TIE UP!

SUSAN — NO! DAMMIT!

'WHAT DO YOU MEAN YOU *LOST* THEM?!'

'ALL THEIR RADIOS AND COMMS WENT DOWN, SIR! WE DON'T KNOW IF THEY'RE ALIVE OR *DEAD*!'

'THEN WE HAVE TO ASSUME SHE *GOT* THEM!'

THAT'S IT! WE HAVE TO GO NUCLEAR! AIM A TEN MEGATON WARHEAD RIGHT AT HER!

NUCLEAR?!

DAMN RIGHT! THERE'S NO OTHER CHOICE!

EVEN SHE CAN'T BE IMMUNE TO THAT! THE ELECTROMAGNETIC PULSE WOULD SCRABLE HER BRAIN!

THAT'S HOW WE KILL HER!

ER, SIR...

AND— AND—

WHAT ARE YOU ALL STARING AT?

OH GOD!

IT'S OKAY! JUST PRETEND THE CAMERA ISN'T HERE AND BE *YOURSELVES*! THIS IS GONNA LOOK GREAT FOR MY DOCUMENTARY!

OH, AND THIS FOOTAGE IS BEING BROADCAST *LIVE* ALL OVER THE WORLD.

187

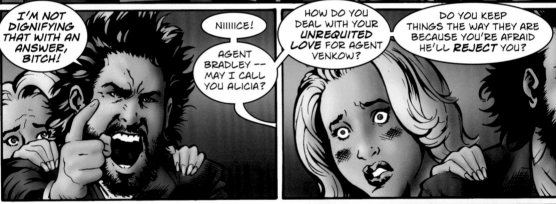

JEEZ! YOU SCREAM LIKE A LITTLE GIRL!

COME ON! MAN UP! TAKE YOUR MEDICINE!

WHU-WHAT ARE YOU GOING TO DO TO ME?

I'M GOING TO GIVE YOU NAOMI-

UUUUUUUUUU!

FUCK YOUR PAPER! YOU GOTTA HELP ME WITH MY OUTFIT FOR THE PARTY!

JEEZ, NAY, IT'S THE 'DRESSED TO GET LAID' PARTY, NOT THE 'DRESS TO FIND THE LOVE OF YOUR LIFE' PARTY!

YOU DON'T KNOW THAT! I GOT MY SIGHTS SET ON A GUY! AND DON'T SAY HE'S NOT THE ONE!

I DUNNO, NAY... YOU DON'T ALWAYS PICK THE GOOD ONES...

YOU ALWAYS PUT DOWN MY CHOICES!

I'M JUST LOOKING OUT FOR YOU.

Chapter 13: **WHEN PARENTS ATTACK!**

MOM! DAD!

WHY ARE YOU **DOING** THIS?

TOOK YOU LONG ENOUGH TO FINALLY REACH YOUR **HIGHER MIND** AGAIN!

NOW WE CAN **PLAY!**

SO YOU TOOK AWAY THE THIRD WORLD PEOPLE'S ABILITY TO BE MURDERED. WHAT ABOUT **EVERYONE ELSE?**

I WAS **GETTING** TO THAT.

YOU'RE GOING TO TURN THE HUMAN RACE **IMMORTAL?**

NOT EXACTLY. JUST **FREE.**

ARE YOU PLANNING TO TURN THEM INTO **US?**

IS THAT EVEN **POSSIBLE?**

WE DON'T WANT TO FIND OUT!

YOU'VE ONLY LIVED FOR TWENTY-FOUR YEARS. WE'VE LIVED **BILLIONS.**

DO YOU KNOW WHAT THAT'S LIKE? THE SLOW, **CRUSHING BOREDOM** AFTER THE FIRST MILLION YEARS?

OUR PEOPLE HAVE BEEN PLAYING GOD WITH WORLDS SINCE FOREVER, AND IT **NEVER** WORKS OUT! THAT'S WHY WE STOPPED!

YOU THINK KILLING THE REST OF OUR PEOPLE WAS **MURDER?** IT WAS AN ACT OF **MERCY!**

YOU–? **WHAT**–?

YOU **KILLED** THEM?!

ALL OF THEM?!

AT LEAST WE DIDN'T HAVE TO WORRY ABOUT LIBBY! SHE DIDN'T *HAVE* ANY POWERS!

AND WE STILL DON'T KNOW *WHY!* WE FOUND NOTHING IN HER MIND!

SUSAN---

LISTEN TO ME...

I KNOW YOU'RE REALLY SCARED NOW... BUT *DON'T* LET THEM GET INTO YOUR HEAD. JUST FOCUS ON MY *VOICE!*

WHAT ARE WE GOING TO DO?

SO HOW SHALL WE DO IT? SHALL WE JUST MAKE THE EARTH'S CORE *OVERHEAT?*

VOLCANOES ERUPT! CITIES BOIL! EVERYBODY BURNS IN ONE *BIG* BARBECUE!

NO!

OR...

STOP IT!

JUST STOP IT, OKAY?

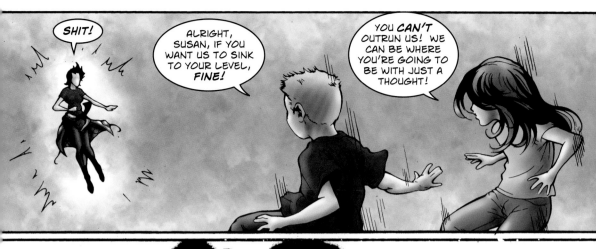

WHEEEE! HEE HEE HEE HEE HEE!

AGAIN! DO IT **AGAIN**!

LISA? FOR HEAVEN'S SAKE! IT'S **TOO EARLY** TO BE MAKING SO MUCH NOISE!

WHAT'S GOING **ON** ANYWAY –?

MUM! LOOK WHO'S **BACK**!

SHE JUST CAME IN THE **WINDOW**!

MISS ME?

I'LL PUT THE KETTLE ON.

SO NO MORE HASSLES, NO MORE PEOPLE TRYING TO KILL YOU OR US, THEN?

NOPE. ALL DONE. EVERYBODY'S *SAFE.*

SO WE'RE FREE AND THE WORLD IS GONNA BE *HUNKY-DORY?* NO MORE CRAZY SHIT?

WELL...

I NEVER WOULD'VE GUESSED YOU KIND OF *HYPNOTIZED* YOURSELF SO YOU DIDN'T KNOW YOU WERE A RECEPTACLE FOR THE HUMAN PSYCHE...

WELL, YOU'VE BEEN CHANNELING THE *HOPES* OF THE HUMAN RACE YOURSELF.

THAT'S WHY I NEVER TRIED TO STOP YOU.

GEE, *THANKS.*

HEY! I CAN GO BACK AND FINISH PUTTING ALL MY *PLANS* INTO PLAY!

SO WHAT DO *YOU* WANT TO DO NOW?

FUCK IT, LET'S TAKE OVER THE WORLD!

SCHADENFREUDE IS A TASTY PIE!

SO IN TWO YEARS, WE'VE SEEN AN END TO TERRORISM, HUMAN TRAFFICKING... WE HAVE GLOBAL UNIVERSAL HEALTHCARE NOW...

YOU REALLY *ENJOYED* KILLING THE HMOS, DIDN'T YOU?

OH YEAH!

HEY! IF YOU SAVE THE WORLD, WHAT DO WE HAVE *LEFT* TO PROTEST?!

NO PERFECT WORLD!

U.S. PREMIERE
TIMES A-CHANGING
A DOCUMENTARY BY SUSAN LA MUSE

SO SUSAN, IT'S BEEN AN *AMAZING* COUPLE OF YEARS!

OH YEAH! I JUST WANTED TO DOCUMENT IT ALL *FIRSTHAND*, YOU KNOW?

EVERYBODY'S CHANGING THE WORLD! ASIA, AFRICA AND THE MIDDLE EAST ARE EVEN MORE PROGRESSIVE AND GREEN THAN THE WEST NOW! PEOPLE ARE GETTING THEIR ACT TOGETHER!

CODA: PLANET LA MUSE

OKAY, ALL OF HUMANITY IS A *CHAOTIC SYSTEM* SET UP TO EVOLVE FROM TRIAL-AND-ERROR. YOU CAN'T SOLVE ALL OF THEIR PROBLEMS FOR THEM.

I KNOW.

I'M JUST GETTING RID OF THE BIGGEST ONES FIRST TO TIP THINGS, *CHANGE THE EQUATION*, THEN LET IT ALL RUN.

WE STEP IN AND *TWEAK* IT EVERY NOW AND THEN.

SO WHAT DO YOU SAY TO THE CHARGES THAT YOU'RE AN ALIEN?

WELL, CELEBRITIES ARE ALIENS.

WE'RE GIVEN A DIFFERENT STATUS. OUR LIFESTYLES ARE DIFFERENT FROM OTHER PEOPLE'S. OUR LIVES BECOME ALIEN ONCE WE BECOME FAMOUS.

WE BECOME A SPECTATOR SPORT.

SUSAN, LIBBY, YOU'RE PRACTICALLY FAMILY, SO, WELL...

FREDDIE AND I WOULD LIKE YOU GUYS TO GIVE US AWAY AT OUR WEDDING.

COOL! WE ARE SO THERE!

WE'D BE HONORED, TIM.

HAD ENOUGH OF THE CELEBRITY GAME YET?

I'M SO BORED. IN TWELVE MONTHS, PEOPLE ARE GONNA FORGET ABOUT ME AND I GO BACK TO OBSCURITY. I'VE GOT IT ALL PLANNED.

THE TRICK TO TAKING OVER THE WORLD IS TO NOT LET ANYONE KNOW YOU'VE DONE IT.

213

THAT'S *ANTISOCIAL BEHAVIOUR*, AND SOCIETY'LL SHUT 'EM DOWN.

SOCIAL DARWINISM! STRING 'EM UP FROM THE LAMPPOSTS!

HANG THE SCHMATAS!

OH, HONEY...

SO THE WORLD IS SAVED, THINGS ARE A LOT BETTER, BUT *SOME* THINGS STAY THE SAME...

AFRICA AND WHAT WE *USED* TO CALL THE THIRD WORLD ARE DOING GREAT ON THEIR *OWN* WITHOUT THE WEST AND THE CORPORATIONS...

OIL IS OVER, AND WE'RE ALL ABOUT CARBON-FREE, RENEWABLE FUELS!

AND NO MORE DICTATORS. NO MORE *GENOCIDE.* 'SALL GOOD.

SO WHAT HAPPENS IF SOMEONE REALLY *BAD* COMES ALONG AGAIN AND *CAN'T* BE REASONED WITH?

THEN I'LL STEP IN.

AFTER ALL, I KNOW WHERE EVERYBODY *LIVES.*

HE'D JERRY-RIGGED THAT **WARHEAD** AND TAPED THE TRIGGER TO HIS HAND! HE WOULDN'T GIVE IT UP UNTIL **YOU** CAME!

VENKOW, DUDE, WHAT'S **UP?**

AT LAST! NOW WE CAN END THIS!

IT'S TIME I RID THE WORLD OF YOU! WE'LL GO OUT TOGETHER!

ER, YEAH, **ABOUT** THAT...

I REGRET NOTHIIIIIING ---!

CLICK!

EEEP?

POP!

...I **DISARMED** EVERY NUKE ON THE PLANET THREE YEARS AGO WHEN NO ONE WAS LOOKING!

SIGH! JUST KILL ME...

NAH. I'LL REPAIR YOUR BRAIN, AND YOU CAN LIVE OUT YOUR DAYS TELLING YOUR STORY. YOU'RE PART OF **HISTORY**, AFTER ALL.

AND BRADLEY **LOVES** YOU. CUT HER SOME SLACK!

TRUTH AND RECONCILIATION! YOU'LL LOVE IT!

I HATE YOU!

I CAN LIVE WITH THAT.

217

SUSAN! SORRY I'M LATE!

HEY, LIB. I WAS JUST CASTING OUT AND LOOKING AT THE FUTURE.

UGH! KNOWING AND NOT KNOWING, ALL THAT QUANTUM SHIT, ALWAYS GIVES ME A HEADACHE.

THAT'S WHY I SENT MY QUANTUM SELF OUTSIDE OF TIME AND SPACE.

BY THE WAY, THAT PROTEIN BLOB I HAD SEX WITH IN SPACE? HUMANITY IS GOING TO MEET ITS DESCENDENTS IN 400,000 YEARS.

BIG SURPRISE!

WE SHOULD BE THERE TO SEE HOW IT TURNS OUT.

FINE!

YOU'RE GONNA HAVE KIDS AND DESCENDENTS, BUT THEY'LL BE NORMAL, NOT LIKE US.

GOOD. DON'T TELL ME WHO THEIR FATHER IS.

BUT YOU ALREADY KNOW. IT'S HAPPENED ALREADY.

I'D RATHER TAKE THE LONG WAY TO KNOW, OKAY?

YOU'RE GONNA LIVE TO ABOUT **200** BEFORE YOU 'PASS AWAY' SURROUNDED BY FAMILY.

SO AT LEAST I GET TO LIVE OUT A **NORMAL** LIFETIME.

ERR... THE THING IS, AFTER YOU DIE, YOUR CELLS WILL **REGENERATE** -- YOU'RE GOING TO BE ALIVE AND **YOUNG** AGAIN.

WHAT? HOW?

I WROTE THAT INTO YOUR **DNA** WHEN I BROUGHT YOU BACK TO LIFE IN THE DESERT.

LOOK, I DON'T THINK I SHOULD BE THE ONLY ONE OF OUR KIND RUNNING **LOOSE** IN THE UNIVERSE. AND I DON'T THINK YOU SHOULD GIVE UP BEING **HUMAN**.

GIVING UP THEIR ORIGINAL BODIES WAS WHAT DROVE MOM AND DAD **NUTS**.

C'MON... IT'LL BE REALLY **TEDIOUS** TO OVER-WRITE YOUR DNA AGAIN.

AND YOUR QUANTUM SELF **HAS** TO REUNITE WITH YOU SOONER OR LATER.

YEAH, YOU'RE RIGHT. IT'S **FINE**.

BUT WE'RE HERE NOW, IT'S A NICE DAY, I CLOSED A DEAL, AND I'M IN THE MOOD FOR A SALADE NIÇOISE.

GOOD IDEA!

WHAT'S THAT YOU'RE READING?

W.B. YEATS. HERE'S A POEM CALLED 'EASTER 1916'.

'ALL CHANGED, CHANGED UTTERLY,'

'...A TERRIBLE BEAUTY IS BORN.'

THAT IS SO YOU.

THANK YOU!

220

END.

About the Creators

Adisakdi Tantimedh's first radio play was commissioned by the BBC at the age of 19, and he has been working as a writer ever since. He has written radio plays and television scripts for the BBC, and screenplays for Hollywood, Britain, and Asia. His script for the short film, "ZINKY BOYS GO UNDERGROUND", co-produced by the BBC and British Film Institute, was shot on location in Russia and won the British Academy of Film and Television Arts award for Best Short Film. He has also written and directed short films that premiered in international film festivals. His past graphic novels include "JLA: AGE OF WONDER" for DC Comics and "BLACKSHIRT" for Moonstone Books. He has a Bachelor of Arts in English Literature and Creative Writing from Bennington College and a Master of Fine Arts in Film and Television Production from New York University. He currently lives and works in New York City.

Hugo Petrus Was born in Menorca, Spain, and has loved comics since reading a Byrne and Giordiano Superman story and the Richard Donner Superman films. He decided to follow his dream of becoming a comic artist after the university, and attended art school (Escola Joso) in Barcelona for three years and learned the basics. His first comics work was a short story for Dark Horse written by Alex de Campi (unpublished), followed by a Dr. Strange custom comic (which was a special insert for the Iron Man DVD). Other works a 4 issue miniseries with John Reppion and Leah Moore, *Rise the Dead,* for Dynamite Entertainment, and two miniseries for the Marvel Illustrated Line: *The Man in the Iron Mask* and *The Three Musketeers*. He was married in June 2008.

-3- spent more than a decade creating art for computer games before retiring to the Pacific Northwest, where he composes advertising art for imported Hong Kong movies and illustrates and colors comics on the side.